Second Sight

by

Kat Green

Haunts for Sale Series, Book Two

Second Sight

Cover Art by *Debbie Taylor*

The Wild Rose Press, Inc.
PO Box 708
Adams Basin, NY 14410-0708
Visit us at www.thewildrosepress.com

Publishing History
First Mainstream Paranormal Edition, 2017
Print ISBN 978-1-5092-1500-3
Digital ISBN 978-1-5092-1501-0

Haunts for Sale Series, Book Two
Published in the United States of America

Dedication

This book is dedicated to both the living and dead…
we are all connected.

Acknowledgments

Rachel and Kat want to thank their paranormal expert, Stephanie Knoff, and their incredible editor, Lill Farrell.

~*~

Rachel would like to thank her amazing friend, Kevin Rodgers, who always reads everything she writes no matter how bad it is. And who also puts smiley faces in his edits to make her smile.

~*~

Kat wants to give a shout out to her amazing street team, *Kat's Pride*, especially Heidi Behm. She also wants to thank her "sensitive" husband…life is better with your soulmate by your side.

Chapter One

Almost sunset in mid-June, Yarmouth, Maine

Brian Monroe squeezed his wife's hand as the real estate agent gave them a final copy of their signed paperwork and slid two sets of house keys across the polished wood desk.

"Congratulations!" The older woman beamed, her eyes crinkling until Brian was sure her makeup would crack. "I'm sure it'll be everything you've dreamt of and more."

"Thank you for all your help," Brian said, shaking the woman's cold clammy hand. "I'm sure it will be."

Climbing into the car beside his wife, Brian couldn't help but smile. They were on their way home at last.

They had scrimped and saved for years before he sold his first hit song and business took off. Moving into record production, his career was soaring, and he was busier than ever. After skimping on dining out while Rin cooked, shopping the sales racks at the discount stores, and going years without a real vacation, he finally felt like they had it all.

A new house.

And a baby on the way.

They'd passed this little slice of heaven hundreds of times on their broke-but-let's-go-on-a-scenic-drive

Sunday's along the Atlantic Coast. No matter this house was a few miles out of the way, Jen always made him take that right turn to catch another glimpse of her dream house. How could he refuse her? The first ultrasound appointment, he was in New York. She'd even called to tell him she was pregnant in the middle of a business conference because she couldn't wait.

Nothing was too good for her, especially if he didn't have the time to spend with her like he used to. A piece of him longed for their old days, spending hours lounging around while he hammered out new riffs on his guitar.

They watched the house change hands, some renovations would begin, and then a new for sale sign would appear. When the place went into foreclosure a few months ago, Rin begged him to walk through it. She practically skipped and danced through every room and her enthusiasm sold him on the place.

"Even the baby loves it!" Rin pulled Brian's hand over her watermelon-cute bump that gave him a firm push.

Life was good.

Tales of a resident spirit made them chuckle, even as they sat at the title company signing their closing papers. He thought of his old high school buddy who was a ghost-hunter. What a nut.

Because the property had a widow's walk, people had long reported seeing an apparition staring out at the restless sea. But Brian and Rin knew widow's walks were frequently found on nineteenth century North American houses. They were romantic, really. The wives of mariners could use the platform to watch for their spouse's ship at sea.

Located just eleven miles northeast of Portsmouth, where Rin's mother still lived, Brian had come to love the quaint area and missed it when work took him across the country. The Atlantic Ocean roared, and the wind skipped across the maple and birch trees surrounding their new home, causing the leaves to rustle like laughter. It sounded like music to him. Modern, dystonic, with time-signatures jumping from measure to measure, but to the former high-school-music-teacher-turned-record-producer, it was music nonetheless. He already had a modern symphony forming in his mind.

"I think this place may inspire me to write music again," he said, opening the door of their SUV for his wife. Brian heard the music of nature, and his brain turned it into symphonies. Staring out at the crashing waves on the beach, he could almost hear dark chords and a haunting melody playing on the wind.

"That's wonderful, Bri." Rin smiled, and Brian had to catch his breath. She was so beautiful with her silky light brown hair and pale skin. Rin wasn't technically an American since she'd been born in Okinawa, Japan. Her father had been stationed there at the time. She'd lived all over the world because of him but moved to Maine in time for her to attend high school.

Hand in hand, they made their way from where they parked at the end of the gravel drive to the white pillared front porch. On a radical whim, old school chivalry overtook him. Brian unlocked the door, pushed it opened, scooped up a giggling Rin, and staggered under her pregnancy weight as he carried her over the threshold into their new life. The sparkle in her eyes was enough motivation for him to sacrifice any of his needs for the rest of his life.

"I had my assistant stock enough food for a week so we don't even have to order out. It's just you and me tonight. I know you want to start working right now, but remember your promise to me? We spend one quiet night here alone and then let the professionals do the rest." He knew it was useless, but he had to try. The look on her face said "give me a dust rag" not "let's relax and listen to the ocean." Ever the compulsive cleaner.

Still in his arms, Rin planted one on his lips before Brian reunited her delicate frame with the hardwood floor. His wallet fell out of his front pocket. Rin lumbered to get it before Brian noticed, and she flipped it open. "I love that you keep our wedding picture where your driver's license should go." Her smile was the same today as it was that day. How a gorgeous brunette could love a man who lost all his hair and shaved his head before he was thirty, was a mystery to him.

Vicious wind howled from the ocean. But he'd sleep in a cardboard box if it meant Rin—the love of his life—was safe and happy.

"We're home," he called out to no one. His voice boomed with an echo into the entryway where a rectangular oriental rug led to a curved staircase. Ten horizontal steps led to an archway that opened into a parlor. White sheets covered the upholstered furniture. The place was sold "as is" which happened to be furnished. The musty smell of mothballs and moldy wood from the fireplace assaulted his nose, but Rin didn't seem to mind. She pulled back thick cream-colored linen drapes to let in the last of the evening sun over the shore. Columns of dust appeared like stairways made of fairy dust.

Bang!

The front door slammed shut.

Rin jumped and pressed her hand over her heart. "Must've been the wind," she murmured.

Brian retrieved their overnight bags from the SUV and dropped them on the carpet with a thud. He unzipped and rifled through his bag, shifting aside real estate papers and pajamas for the bottle of sparkling white grape juice nicely packaged to look like wine, purchased just for this celebration, and two glasses he'd careful stowed away for tonight. With the last rays of the sun pushing through the western sky, Brian uncorked the bottle and poured them each a glass before Rin came back from the kitchen with several small bowls and a bottle of vinegar.

"What in the world are you doing?" he asked.

Rin carefully poured vinegar into the bowls and placed them on the windowsills. "This will soak up the musty smell. Trust me." She winked.

He lit candles as he moved through the home: the Victorian living room with the wood-carved fireplace. The wine-themed kitchen where he hoped to spend long hours sipping Merlot and the dining room with the antique tin ceiling. Then upstairs past the master bedroom to the small corner room that would one day be the nursery. He lit a lavender candle and spent two minutes in the rocking chair, his heart warm with the idea of his growing family.

Rin poked her head in. "What are you doing?"

"Just dreaming. I thought you were de-musting. Are you done?"

Rin nodded, still distracted. "Give me five minutes, sweetie."

"Okay." Deciding to make a quick walk-through of the upstairs, Brian noticed something he hadn't on any of the showings. At the top of the landing, a small phrase was stenciled on the wall: "Those who cannot remember the past are condemned to repeat it.—George Santayana," he read aloud.

In the same moment when he was convinced they'd purchased the perfect house, the air thickened, and his ears felt as if they would pop, like he was in an elevator at the top of a skyscraper and dropping fast. A rush of cool air passed by him causing an instant ice-cream type headache. His temples throbbed.

Had something just moved past him?

The hair on his whole body went to full alert, and his heart began thumping. He had a terrible sinking feeling that he wasn't alone.

A tap on his shoulder.

An indiscernible whisper.

"Rin?" He swung around.

A black mass—darker than the darkness around him—rushed past him and into the master bedroom.

"I'm ready," Rin called from downstairs.

"Just a minute," he called back to her. Logic told him to run, but common sense told him this was nothing. He followed whatever it was into the master bedroom flipping on the light, his gaze searching the room. The furniture was sparse—a bed and a table against the wall between the dormer windows. The rest of the room was empty.

Across from the bed was an open doorway. He leaned through the frame to switch on the light, and his own reflection greeted him. The master bathroom. Just a standing shower, a blue porcelain toilet (which would have to go) and a matching sink with cabinets below. Hanging over the sink, a large rectangular mirror took up most of the wall, giving him a good look at his pale face. The looking glass was framed with antique bronze scrollwork around the edges. The edges were mottled with small black spots, the rest of the glass hazy, showing its age. He swallowed twice giving his brain a second to process what just happened.

He was overtired from the stress of work and the sale. That must be it.

Imagining things.

Things he shouldn't bother telling Rin about in her delicate condition.

Still…it was an old house. One of the oldest in town. And those rumors…

Coming out of the bathroom, he checked all around the master bedroom one more time but didn't see anything odd. It must have been his imagination. He started for the door, intending to find his wife, when a dark mass rushed from behind the bed into the bathroom.

"What the hell…" He turned to follow as Rin waddled into the room. She giggled with the joy of a three-year old on Christmas morning. She leaned in, kissing him softly then laid her head on his shoulder. "I'm so excited, Bri! I love this place." She sighed, her breath tickling his ear. "I know this will be where all our dreams come true, and we'll live until our dying day!"

The look in her eyes and the excitement in her smile drove the fear from his mind.

"Rin, I…"

"Hang on a sec, I have to use the restroom." She headed into the bathroom.

"Wait a sec." He reached for her.

"It'll just be minute, silly. You know how it is. I feel like this is all I do right now with the baby coming so soon."

"Ok, but hurry." He let go of her arm, and she laughed as she went into the old bathroom.

"I swear, you've been so protective since I got pregnant." She laughed. "Girls can take care of themselves. And you better remember that when our daughter is here."

"Son," he called back. They hadn't found out the sex, wanting it to be a surprise. He honestly didn't care what it was, he just liked bickering with her about it.

He crossed the room to the old bed. It had been aired out and the sheets changed. He'd had his assistant deal with that. He'd told her to stock the kitchen and make sure it was clean and to freshen the master bedroom. It wasn't like anything was staying anyway. The contractors were coming next week, and the whole place would look different the next time they were here. That's why Rin had wanted this one night when it was still old.

Relaxing, he lay back on the bed, crossing his arms behind his head.

The slamming of a door and an ear-piercing shriek of terror froze the blood in his veins.

"Rin!" He was across the room in an instant, wrenching at the glass knob.

The door was locked.

And Rin was still screaming.

Brian reacted without rational thought, kicking and pounding on the door as he yelled her name. He threw his shoulder at the door, trying to barrel through like a cop on TV. Nothing he did mattered. The door wouldn't budge.

"Rin! Rin! Please, Rin!" He slumped against the wood, his breath coming in sharp, painful rasps as he sobbed.

Abruptly the screaming stopped, giving way to silence. With an audible click, the lock released and the door creaked open on its own. Brian froze in the doorway.

In the center of the mirror was a dark hole ringed in a bright red light. And his wife was being pulled into the hole. All he could see of Rin was her feet sticking out the hole.

Brian lunged, latching onto her ankle.

Fire burned up his arms as if he'd stuck them into an open flame. He cried out in agony but refused to release his hold on his wife. She kept sinking further, disappearing into the mirror until he had nothing to hold onto. She slipped out of his grasp, and he collapsed on the cold tile floor as his wife disappeared into the mirror.

Chapter Two

Sloane Osborne leapt out of bed with the echo of her own scream roaring through her head like a pair of F-16 fighter jets doing a fly by. Pain shot from the back of her neck down both arms. Her hands were clammy and numb.

Dammit! I'm not dying. I'm thirsty, she repeated to herself over and over.

Water.

That word had taken on all kinds of new meaning since the time she spent in Alvin Mitchell's torture chamber of a basement. She never wanted to go through anything like that again. Gunshots. Screaming. Women on fire. Decaying skin, exposed bones, death and…thirst.

Stop it! Taking steady, deep breaths, she stumbled to her small apartment's kitchen where she slammed one of the dozens of bottles of water strategically stockpiled throughout her home. She'd already finished the three she had in her room. After another eight ounces, she glanced at the clock on the microwave. Four a.m. She'd been asleep for less than an hour.

Knees shaking, she ripped the foil off an antihistamine her pharmacist said would help her sleep and wondered if the small pink oval pill could really make her calm enough to get some shut eye.

She jumped when the music of Michael Jackson's

10

Thriller echoed from the kitchen table.

She needed to change Jonah's ringtone.

Fumbling though her purse, she pulled out a wad of tissue, two half full water bottles, a lip balm, and a stack of business cards that read:

"Sloane Osborne. Paranormal Investigator and Real Estate Agent:

I am in the business of selling haunted houses."

Sloane had been a paranormal investigator before her fiancé died. After getting her real estate license, she'd combined the professions.

By the time she located her phone on the table next to her purse, she'd missed his call. For half a minute she debated not calling him back. If she called him, she'd never get back to sleep. And he'd been on her case to get out more lately. But she knew better than to ignore him. He'd hound her if she didn't call.

She hit one. His was the only number on speed dial.

"Avoiding me again?" He didn't even bother to say hello. She didn't hold it against him. They were beyond that by now.

"No, I couldn't find my phone. How did you know I was awake?" She sat in her one and only kitchen chair, leaning back so the chair stood on two legs. She balanced her feet on the table.

"Sloane, we're connected. Haven't you figured that out by now?" He sighed, and she could hear the resignation in his voice. As if he was tired of repeating the same thing over and over again.

He was right. They *were* connected. He'd proved that last year when he saved her life. He could sense things about her and vice-versa. Sometimes it was nice to have someone know you that well.

"Nightmare again?" he asked.

"Do I need to answer?" she responded. "Just once I'd like to get eight hours of sleep. Hell, I'd settle for three consecutive hours. I don't even care when, as long as it's sleep."

"Your psychiatrist told you this would happen." He sighed. "I wish it were different, but you've suffered a severe trauma."

"Gone a little crazy, you mean." Sloane picked up a piece of her long hair, examining it for split ends.

"You're not crazy," Jonah insisted. "If you were, I wouldn't be your friend anymore. I'd commit you and be done with it."

Sloane smiled. Jonah could always make her smile.

"You're working too hard though," Jonah continued. "You need a break."

"I can't take a break. There's no stopping me now. I'm on a roll. I sold three houses last month alone. Who would have thought almost dying would get me so many clients?"

The untapped market for legit haunted houses blew her mind. People were willing to fly her anywhere for a few nights stay before they signed on the dotted line. Especially with all the publicity she'd gotten for uncovering a mass murderer.

"Listen to me, Sloane." Jonah's voice took on the tough edge she imagined he used for interrogation at the FBI. "You are taking a break from the home sale business."

"Don't talk to me like that, Mr. High-And-Mighty." Sloane wasn't about to let him get away with it. "I'm not the boobilicious underling you call a partner. You can't order me around."

"You're right, Sloane," Jonah said. "I give up. I'm not your keeper. But can I ask a favor?"

"You want *my* help?" How could she help him? "And how is my helping you giving me a break?"

"It's not a break, per se… And, well, it's not really for me, but one of my old friends. He's in Maine…"

"No, you already sent me to Maine, remember? It was right after the…incident." Sloane didn't really like talking about her time in Wisconsin, but sometimes it was unavoidable. "I seem to remember I sold a very nice Cape Cod to a couple moving in from California. And there was also a resident spirit who likes making pictures hang crooked and standing too close to the TV. It was a nice, easy sale and a fun, playful spirit."

"Yes, but this time it's in Yarmouth," Jonah replied. "I think this ghost might have a slightly different temperament. And it would be a favor for my old friend, Brian."

"Brian Monroe? The guy who used to play in that awful band you and Michael liked?" She leaned her hip against the counter, reaching for a handful of walnuts. She read somewhere they were supposed to help you sleep.

"The same."

"But didn't he make it big and become some kind of music guy?" Sloane asked.

"Seriously, do you ever read the news?" Jonah laughed out loud, a warm chuckle that made her heart flutter.

In fact, Sloane recalled something about Brian Monroe becoming a music producer and signing a new band that was making tons of money, but she liked to annoy Jonah.

"He won a Grammy last year for music production, Sloane." She could hear him grinding his teeth.

"Yeah, yeah, I know who he is," she admitted. "But it's four a.m., and you are the one who called me."

"He bought this house in Maine for his wife, Rin. She was a military brat. Lived all over. Came here when she was in high school and she was raised near Yarmouth. They used to take Sunday drives, and since the first time she saw the house, she wanted to live there. It's been vacant on and off for years. They finally got pregnant, and he bought it for her."

"How sweet." Sloane tried to keep the sarcasm out of her voice. She knew she was becoming the embittered crone she dreaded, but she'd dreamt of a family once. She and Michael had wanted a house full of kids. Only he was dead and that dream died with him. "But what does it have to do with me? They already bought the house."

"According to Brian, there's something *in* the house," Jonah said. "Brian called me hysterical last night. Rin had told him town rumors she didn't believe about how the house was haunted. But he said that on the first night they were going to stay there, his wife was pulled through the bathroom mirror. And he hasn't seen her since."

"Wait, you think this case sounds like a break for me?" Sloane interrupted. "It's not. First of all, are the police involved since this is a missing person? Second, and more importantly, do *you* believe him?"

"He called me asking for a professional to come investigate," Jonah continued. "He can't tell anyone else because he barely believes his own words. Right now, he's just out of his mind with worry. But it's more than that. What he hasn't thought of is the publicity. He's a high-profile figure. If the media gets wind that she's missing, they're going to blast it all over the place. And from the story he's telling me, he's going to be the one and only suspect."

"His wife disappeared into a mirror?" Sloane couldn't keep the disbelief from her voice. She remembered Brian. He'd been drunk or high for most of their third year. She had no idea how he'd managed to graduate. "Are you serious? Like Alice in Wonderland?"

"After she'd been missing twenty-four hours, she officially became a missing person. That's when they'll bring him in for questioning. They can hold him up to seventy-two hours without evidence. That buys you a little time. Besides, Brian asked for you by name. He remembered you from college. Don't make me beg, Sloane. Because I will. I love the guy, but this is strange, even for him. We both know how he was. I thought he'd changed, but now I'm not sure what to think. Maybe Rin couldn't handle him anymore and left him, but Brian is in denial or something. Whatever happened, it needs to be figured out quick. He's in real trouble."

She swallowed as her sixth sense clicked on. The house was almost calling to her. "Of course I'll go, but isn't it a crime scene? What do you expect me to do? I'm not a cop or anything."

"Just do what you do best and see if there is some sort of vindictive spirit there. I pulled some strings to get you past the red tape, but you only have a few days. Your flight is at nine. I'll fax you the paperwork granting you access to observe and investigate the site right now."

****

Yarmouth's quaint downtown was only fourteen miles from the Portland International Jetport, and Sloane enjoyed the wind in her hair as she took the scenic route down Princes Point Road in the bright red convertible rental she'd upgraded to. Brian would be paying, of course. Or maybe Jonah. She'd love to see his face when he got the bill.

The air tasted of salt and sea. She could hear the crashing waves even before the ocean came into view on the long winding drive to Brian's new house. She parked near the front and took in the view. She listened to the rustle of the wind on the beach and the roar of the surf, but the old house seemed to call out to her, like it wanted her to enter. And how could she disappoint it?

The bungalow style home had a lovely wraparound porch complete with a set of rocking chairs she found herself drawn to. She climbed the steps and took a seat, leaning back and relaxing for a moment. Whitewashed with black trim and accents, the home had a lot of curb appeal even if the landscaping was overgrown and unkempt and the lawn needed a thorough weeding. It even sported a turret of some kind. A widow's walk. Like a mini one-person lookout for ships on the horizon. Immediately, the place appealed to her. Until another emotion hit her…hard.

Loneliness.

Maybe it was the pair of rocking chairs. Or the vast sandy beach stretching in both directions. Or the rhythmic crashing of the surf as if begging for a lover's hand in hand stroll. Something tugged at her in places she deemed nonexistent after Michael's death.

A vast emptiness or hole only another living person could fill.

A mild jealously rose within her for Brian and Rin. Growing old side by side rocking away each evening, staring at the ocean. Sloane paid a hefty price for falling in love. She'd known the sweet taste of a first kiss, melting into the blush of first love, then simmering into a relationship that's made to stand the test of time.

She'd had that, and she'd lost it all in one afternoon.

She could still remember bits and pieces of that day. There was the joy she'd felt that they were finally going to get that one last piece, the marriage license. Then there was the noise. The screeching tires, the crunch of metal slamming into metal and bending until it broke. And after that, the loneliness and the guilt.

Why is he gone and I'm left here alone?

She'd struggled with that every day. How was the world a better place with Michael dead and her alive?

And now there was the guilt for the little whispering voice in the back of her head reminding her she belonged to Michael when she was beginning to acknowledge her feelings for Jonah.

Could she really dishonor Michael's memory by having a relationship with his best friend? No matter. His job would always keep them apart. Sure he was there in an emergency, but day to day she was getting used to being alone.

She blinked and brought herself back to reality. How long had she been sitting staring idly at the ocean?

Goosebumps rose on her arms as the air chilled around her. Sloane held her breath, not daring to move.

There was something there with her.

"Hello?" she said. "You don't have to hide. I know you're here."

The rocking chair next to her began to move.

Had the wind pushed it? She stood and edged away from the pair of rockers meant for lovebirds. The one she'd used stood still but the one next to it rocked to and fro, quickly, as if the occupant was agitated.

"I'm Sloane. I want to help you. But first I need you to tell me what happened to Rin."

The chair stopped moving, and Sloane heard a soft growl next to her ear. She turned her head, but nothing was there. Her heart stuttered in her chest. Sometimes Sloane wondered why she enjoyed her job so much. Maybe it was this fear factor. That something she couldn't see could reaching out from the other side. Touching her. Even hurting her.

Without warning, the piece of furniture flew through the air, slamming into the porch railing next to where she was standing.

Sloane stared at the chair for a moment, wondering how much damage it would have done if she'd been standing two inches to the right. *Holy crap!* She pressed a hand over her chest to convince her heart to stop frantically palpitating. Once the chill left and she was alone once again, she picked up the rocker, putting it back where it belonged. This *was* a haunting. And not an innocent one. Her brain told her to leave, check into a hotel, and wait for Jonah to call. But her adrenaline junkie side, said, *"Fun! Stay the night. See what happens."*

She tried the front door. Locked. Jonah had texted her to say that a neighbor would be there to let her into the house. What was the woman's name? Laura? Or Nora? She couldn't remember.

Sloane now needed to collect tangible proof of this haunting and figure out exactly what she was dealing with. Clearly, something had happened inside this place with Brian and Rin. But was Rin really missing? Sloane didn't have the luxury of time, Jonah had managed to hold the investigation off because of his connections, but in a few days, this place would be torn apart by police looking for evidence. Of foul play.

As if Jonah was watching over her from Washington D.C., her phone buzzed with a message from him.

Brian said to tell you if the neighbor doesn't show, he thinks there's a hide-a-key taped under the front mat.

Perfect. Sloane bent over to retrieve the key.

When she reached up to slide the key into the lock, she noticed the door was slightly ajar. Hadn't it just been locked? Her heart racing, she pushed it gently, peering inside. A white-haired lady in frumpy faded blue flower dress that fell just below her knees and light yellow apron was standing in the entry. "Hello?" she asked, friendly lines circling her hazel eyes.

"Hi, I'm Sloane. I'm staying here for a few nights. Brian told me someone would be here to let me in. I didn't see anyone, so I got the hidden key. Sorry if I frightened you."

The old woman's wrinkled skin stretched into a huge grin, and she made the universal "come on in" sign. "Welcome, welcome. I've been expecting you, sweetie. Are you hungry? So sorry, I'm Flora."

Sloane pulled the door shut behind her with some

effort as the wind fought against her in what she assumed must be a daily tug of war. Wrinkling her nose against the sharp tang of dust and mold, she willed herself not to sneeze. She could see the charm of the place even in the entryway: crown molding and the tin tiles on the ceiling. Scrolled woodwork leading up a thick staircase. Nice to finally be in a house she didn't have to stage for an open house, just explore.

"The house is a bit messy really," the neighbor said. "I've been trying to clean it for them."

Maybe not the best idea if the place turns into a crime scene. But Sloane had more than enough reason to know something unusual was going on around here. "Flora, can you tell me, aren't there some old rumors about this place? Like it's haunted? Aren't you frightened here all alone?" Sloane asked.

Flora laughed. "Frightened? Of what? People love stories of things going bump in the night. But that's all hogwash. And it sounds like that nice couple will be back in a few days, so I offered my services to them. Cleaning up, that sort of thing." She turned to Sloane after she reached the kitchen and sat down at the table. "I hope they stay. They didn't say they were scared of this place, did they? I don't get into town much anymore, and it's going to be nice having them to talk to. Sometimes, it gets pretty lonely out here for me."

Sloane's heart went out to the woman. If her parents were alive, and one of them still lived in her childhood home, she'd like to know they had nice neighbors around, too. Just in case. "Well, you'll have me to talk to for the next few days. I do have some equipment to bring in and set up, but I can do that later. Would you mind terribly if I asked you a few questions about this place?"

"Of course I wouldn't mind," Flora said, adding, "Would you like some tea?"

Sloane nodded, finally taking some time to look around the kitchen. She liked the décor immediately. It was simple, yet tasteful. A wine theme. A vineyard painted on one wall, pictures of grapes and even stools behind the kitchen island made from refurbished wine barrels. Sloane pulled out a small notebook and a pencil from her purse.

"How long have you lived in Yarmouth?" Sloane asked.

"All my life dear. Most of the men around these parts made their living fishing. Looking for the lobster bugs and the quahogs and steamer clams. Maybe a tuna or two if they were lucky."

"You said before this house has a reputation for going bump in the night. What did you mean by that?"

"All houses have history," Flora said, clasping her hands in front of her. "This one more than most, I guess. The whole town knows the history. Last time I counted there was pert near a dozen deaths in this house. But that's to be expected in a house that's almost one hundred and fifty years old. In all those years, someone could have decided to stay around."

"Were there any violent deaths?" Sloane asked.

"What a question." Flora put a hand to her heart. "Do you mean was anyone murdered?"

"Murder, suicide, a strange or unexplained accident." Sloane shrugged. "The result is still the same."

"I don't think I can handle this kind of talk without a warm tea in my hand," Flora said. "Why don't I get started on that?"

"I'll do it." Sloane got up. She needed to keep the woman talking, and if she wanted tea, she'd get tea. "So something did happen?"

"Not here." The older woman heaved a sigh, going to the window and looking out at the sea. "But I've heard the story before. It's popular in this part of the state. Have you ever heard of the term widow's walk?"

"I know what it is, but I'm not sure where the term came from." Sloane shook her head, leaning against the counter. She was no closer to starting this accursed tea. She wracked her brain. She needed a teapot of course. Hot water. Tea bags and what did people put in tea? She'd stall. Maybe the woman would answer her questions and head home without the warm, tasteless beverage that Sloane was clueless on how to expertly produce.

"In reality it's just a railed rooftop platform," Flora chatted happily, "purely for decoration, but the truth is women would stand up there, watching for their husbands to come home from sea. Many women came to realize upon those walkways when a storm came up and their loved ones didn't return, that they were now alone. That's why it's called a widow's walk. And sometimes, when a woman couldn't handle the loss, one step off the side would end her pain."

"I saw one on this house, didn't I?" Sloane asked. It's good she wasn't on a widow's walk when she found out Michael died. She woke up in the hospital. But if anyone understood grief, it was her. And a pretty big piece of her even understood why a woman would jump.

"Yes, there are lots of homes on the coast that have

one, but most have never been used for that dreadful purpose. Some talk of seeing a woman on the widow's walk of this house if that helps your little investigation. But I've never seen anything of the sort. So what do you do, sweetie? Are you some kind of ghost hunter or something?"

Sloane sighed, running a hand though her hair. She needed a shower, but that would have to wait. She'd have to settle for washing her face.

"Yeah, I guess you could say that. And what you've told me about the place helps a lot. Say, Flora, I've had quite the long day. Can we have tea tomorrow? Right now, I think I'm going to head upstairs and freshen up before I lug the rest of my stuff inside," Sloane said.

"Absolutely, my dear. I have plenty to do. Go ahead and choose an upstairs bedroom. There are four!" Flora exclaimed, sounding impressed.

Sloane lugged her bag upstairs and chose a small, furnished bedroom. Not able to wait a minute longer, she went to check out the master bedroom, aka, Brian's "source of the abduction." It was bright, full of late afternoon sunshine. She crossed the wooden floor and opened the door to the bathroom. Poking her head inside, she looked around. It was smaller than she'd expected. There weren't any windows and barely enough room to hang a towel on the wall. The floor was white and the walls papered in large gaudy pink and yellow flowers interspersed with green leaves. There was a blue toilet, shower, and sink. The mirror was foggy and pitted on the edges with age. No portal to hell in here, at least not right now. Actually, the inside of the house really didn't feel at all out of the ordinary.

If the rocking chair incident hadn't happened, Sloane would be inclined to think Brian was delusional. Nothing spooky about the *inside* of this place yet. Although drafty and loud from the continual roar of the ocean, the house actually felt cozy and well-loved. But it wasn't nighttime either. Everything can change in the night.

Sloane leaned closer to the mirror, letting her breath fog on the glass. Using one finger, she drew a picture of a cartoon ghost on the glass. Still nothing. The hairs on the back of her neck were still behaving. Brian had always been a bit of a trickster, and he'd never believed in Sloane or Jonah's stories about the supernatural. He was the kind of guy who pushed the planchette across the Ouija board but insisted he didn't. This story about his wife being pulled into the mirror was a little much, even for Brian. But Sloane knew whatever was outside might have access to the inside of the house as well. Better to never underestimate anything being possible. Jonah had told her time and time again, "Assume the worst and you might stay alive. Get complacent and you're dead."

After changing and splashing some water on her face, Sloane heard "Good night, dear!" and the front door slam. She probably should have let Flora out, but the woman was obviously a good friend of Brian and Rin's already, and if they trusted her with a key, then so be it. Sloane set to hauling in her equipment and set up her nerve center, then tripods in the upstairs hall way, bedrooms, bathroom, and parlor.

Just when her work was almost done, there was an impatient rapping on the front door. Sighing in resignation, Sloane opened the door to find a quartet of people with shirts that all read the same thing: "Yarmouth Ghost Hunters Society."

Great...

Chapter Three

There were five of them, but there may as well have been a hundred.

"Hi." A woman so short she could have been a child stuck out a pudgy hand, and Sloane felt forced to take it. She was small, but the scowl lines around her mouth said she was at least in her mid-thirties.

The woman didn't let go as she launched into her sales pitch. "You must be the new owner. It's a pleasure to make your acquaintance."

"I'm not the owner," Sloane cut in. "I'm a friend of the owner. Sloane Osborne."

"Wait, *the* Sloane Osborne?" The woman put her other hand to her chest, her jaw dropping as if she was in shock. "As in the paranormal real-estate agent?"

"Um…yeah…that's me." Sloane knew she looked confused. Anyone would be if their name was suddenly recognized like they were a celebrity.

"You're famous in the paranormal world, you know," she continued, still shaking Sloane's hand. "We heard all about you and the little incident in Wisconsin. All of us here at the Yarmouth Ghost Hunting Society are very glad to see you looking so healthy and hydrated."

"Uh…thanks?" Sloane wasn't sure how else to respond to that.

"I'm Bess—Bess L., that is." She spoke so fast it

made Sloane's head spin. "And this is Bess C. We're the co-presidents."

A sickeningly, skinny woman with fluffy brown hair waved her fingers, flashing blood-red nails. Sloane had heard of the walking dead, but this woman took it to new levels. Her arms were as thin as Sloane's middle finger, a finger she was about to show them if they didn't leave her alone. She reminded her of the Skeletor bad guy from a show she used to watch as a kid. Skeletor-a! That was perfect. She stifled a giggle and tried not to stare.

The tiny lady was babbling again. Talking about something to do with ghosts or maybe it was the town, but Sloane couldn't concentrate. She'd never liked the name Bess. Conjured up images of cows chewing on cud. She watched the short woman talk, not registering a word the girl was saying, but watching her lips move. It did remind her a lot of a cow.

Sloane was starting to feel sick to her stomach and tried to pull her hand away. The first Bess held on tight.

"…and the society has simply flourished under our leadership. Quite an accomplishment, don't you think?" Tiny Bess paused, and Sloane searched for a response.

"Yes, of course." Sloane hoped she hadn't agreed to something important.

"We're up to nine members now," Skeletora Bess gushed.

"Impressive," Sloane said, unimpressed. "The paranormal society I started in only had thirty members, so I know how hard it is to keep your numbers up. It was nice of you to stop by." Sloane managed to pull her hand away as she made to shut the door, but Bess number two put out an emaciated hand, blocking her from closing the front door.

"We knew you'd understand," Tiny Bess turned to her partner in crime. "Didn't I tell you just last night, Bess? This was meant to be. I could *feel* it."

Obviously they'd missed the sarcasm lacing Sloane's words. And now they wanted to work with her? Sloane felt a headache starting in the middle of her forehead. Another few minutes with these two and she knew she'd develop a slight twitch in her right eye, too. Great.

Now Skeletora stuck out her hand for a shake. How was she going to get them to leave? She bobbed their hands up and down together, Sloane unable to disentangle from her tenacious grasp. The woman held on like a suckerfish! To really push her boundaries, she finally wiggled her rail thin body past Sloane and stepped inside the house uninvited.

"So, let me introduce you to the rest of the group I brought out today," she continued, finally releasing Sloane from her death grip now that she'd made it in the house. "You've already met Bess L. The handsome one carrying all the *heavy* equipment is Hank—he's mine so don't get any ideas."

Tiny wiggled her ring finger, showing off a rock the size of her hand. Her laugh was wicked, like someone who'd also laugh while she skipped you in line at the coffee shop and stepped on your foot in the process.

"The others are Whitney and Kevin. They're new." She flipped one hand dismissively at the other two people she'd brought. Sloane decided she liked the new kids better than the rest of the group already. Anyone who got a dismissive wave as an introduction was someone to befriend. Besides, the "newbies" stared at the pair of Besses with such disdain she knew they had actual thoughts running through their heads instead of the brainless twitter going on in the heads of Tiny Bess and Skeletora.

Tiny's "man," Hank, pursed his lips as he looked Sloane up and down. His head to toe appraisal made her feel dirty but she stared back at him. He may have been handsome, with his slicked-back hair and the dimple in his chin, but he did nothing for Sloane. From the muscles bulging under his pale pink polo, he must work out, but his pot belly said he probably indulged in a few too many beers at the local pub.

Then again, Sloane had only been around his significant other for two and a half minutes, and she needed a drink.

The one introduced as Whitney looked like someone Sloane could drink with, if the girl was old enough to drink. The girl's big blue eyes were rimmed in black, making them stand out. She had a riot of shoulder length red hair and a baby face, but her sardonic expression told Sloane there was a sense of humor in there. She jutted out a hip to lean against the porch railing, her eyes meeting Sloane's for a moment. She raised her brows as if to say, "good-luck."

The "newbie" guy was a little older and hung to the back of the group as if he knew he didn't belong. Sloane wanted to go stand with him. He was tall with a mop of curly brown hair and a short goatee. His demeanor was tentative, but Sloane felt herself thinking if the man would take off the coke-bottle glasses, he might be cute.

Tiny Bess clapped her hands like a school teacher.

"Let's get started then. Bess, how about you set up an infrared camera in the bedroom?" She headed up the narrow staircase, giving orders as she moved. "And a microphone for sound."

"Excuse me," Sloane said. "You can't do that." A piece of her wanted to send both Besses to the haunted bathroom and see if something would pull them into a vortex.

"But we can. You see, we've talked to the owner and have permission to run our tests." Skeletora spoke slowly, her tone condescending, as though Sloane wasn't smart enough to understand.

"Brian gave you permission?" This was news to Sloane.

"No, his wife," Skeletora said, but the look she shared with Tiny only proved the statement to be a lie.

"Well, if you've talked to Rin, that's no problem then. Just call her and have her tell me it's okay and you're in. Do you have her number?" Sloane crossed her arms over her chest. A nice test. If she answered, she was not in another dimension and hadn't been pulled into a mirror. If she didn't answer…well.

"I might have an e-mail," Tiny said.

"E-mails don't work," Sloane said. "They're too easily faked. I need to talk to Rin or Brian, or there's no way I'm letting you near this investigation."

"Ok, so we don't exactly have permission." Tiny put on her sweetest smile. Sloane felt like smacking it right off her little face. She didn't have time for this. "I spoke to Rin last week when we were seated next to each other at Prizano's, and I couldn't help but introduce myself."

"I'm sure you couldn't," Sloane said under her

breath. She wasn't sure if Tiny had heard her or not because she continued talking without missing a beat.

But Whitney's smirk widened. Sloane was almost angry at how amusing the girl thought her misery was. Then again, she'd be doing the exact same thing if the roles were reversed.

"I told her about out little group and how long we've wanted to see if the rumors about this house were true," Tiny prattled on. "She told me if she bought the house I could come over any time I wanted to check the place out."

"That seems like a credible story," Sloane said.

"So we can stay?" Skeletora jumped up and down in a mini-celebration.

"Of course you can," Sloane said, putting on a sweet smile of her own. "As soon as you have written permission signed by the owner and notarized by an official."

"Ha!" Whitney clapped a hand over her mouth attempting to hold in her mirth.

"You be quiet over there," Tiny snapped.

"Sorry," Whitney spoke up for the first time. "It's just that I told you this wouldn't work."

Sloane thought she could get to like this Whitney girl. She had spunk. Maybe she would make a good partner? Jonah *was* always nagging her about getting one of those, and after what had happened in Wisconsin, she was beginning to think he was right. Not that she'd ever admit it to him.

"Fine, then." Skeletora huffed, placing one hand on her skinny hip and shaking a finger at Sloane. "We'll leave as soon as you show us *your* paperwork."

The smirk on her face told Sloane the stupid

woman actually thought she'd won. Skeletora didn't think Sloane had paperwork either.

Boy, was she happy to prove them wrong.

Sloane never made a move without making sure everything was in writing. She always insisted on having her t's crossed and her i's dotted. It was a good habit to have in the real estate business. Digging through her black hole of a purse, Sloane produced a letter from Brian Monroe requesting her services and a notarized contract between them granting her exclusive live-in rights until the matter was closed. Jonah knew enough to make sure she had this in her hands before she'd even gotten on the plane.

"Anything else?" Sloane asked. She hated dissing the local paranormal team, but this was her gig. And a high paying gig at that. If there really was a dangerous portal in this house, she was not going to take responsibility for these amateurs getting sucked into another dimension.

Tiny folded her arms over her chest, pouted out her bottom lip, and Sloane was pretty sure she saw tears form in those big brown eyes. She stalked outside, slamming the screen door behind her.

"We'll get inside this house," Skeletora said, flipping her fluffy hair over her shoulder and sticking her long nose in the air. "Just you wait. You'll be begging for our help before you know it!"

Hank, the poor man who was married to one of the Besses—Sloane had already forgotten which one—picked up the bags he'd lugged to the front porch and retreated as well.

The new kids lingered behind the rest. "I'm so sorry," the redhead said, shouldering an expensive-looking tripod and video camera. "They insisted on coming over here. And don't let them fool you. They have spies everywhere. They probably knew you were coming to town before your plane landed. They were so sure you'd say yes to them. Said you'd have no trouble working with a group."

"I *have* worked with groups," Sloane said. "And I've learned the importance of safety in numbers, but I'm not sure your ghost hunting society is the right fit for this case."

"It's not really our fit either." Kevin took off his coke-bottle glasses to clean the lenses on the bottom of his white t-shirt. Sloane's guess had been right. He was good looking without the geeky glasses. "But there aren't a lot of options in Yarmouth. You have to travel to a bigger city to find a real paranormal investigation team."

After the Besses and their brute slammed their car doors and roared out of the driveway, Sloane started to feel a little more camaraderie with these two. She'd been just like them once—eager for hard evidence. Something concrete to prove to the world they weren't crazy. In fact, these two reminded her a little bit of how she and Jonah used to be.

"I'll tell you what," Sloane heard herself say before she'd thought it through. "I just got here and haven't even gotten settled yet. Give me some time to see what's going on, and if you're still interested, I'll let you come by and test out that fancy equipment you're totting around."

"That would be wonderful." Whitney grinned. "We wouldn't be in the way. I promise."

"Just you two," Sloane rushed to say. "Not the rest

of your group."

"Of course," Whitney said. "We won't even mention it to them."

"Here's my card." Sloane pulled one out of her bag. "Give me a call."

"We will." Kevin glanced out the window. "C'mon Whitney, let's get out of her way. Before the others come back and realize we've seceded from the union. You know what I mean?"

"Thanks again." Whitney stuck the card in her back pocket. "I'll be in touch."

Once everyone was gone, Sloane felt better. She was used to working alone anyhow.

Puttering around, she finished setting up her equipment, but her heart wasn't in it. The loneliness she'd felt when she'd arrived struck again, and she found herself wandering upstairs and taking the circular stairway to the widow's walk on top of the house, even though she wasn't sure the stairs were structurally sound.

The walk was clean, swept free of all debris, which was odd. The rest of the house had a layer of dust an inch thick and a musty smell, like an old kitchen rag.

Sloane leaned over the wrought iron rail and gazed out at the sea. The moon was up. Its light reflected on the distant waves. It was time to work, but Sloane couldn't make herself move.

She stared at the ring on her left hand, twirling the diamond around and around her finger with her thumb. It was a nervous habit and could be the reason she hadn't taken it off.

No.

I'm lying to myself. I can't let Michael go.

Even though she'd made contact with his ghost and said a final good-bye, she couldn't do it.

When she finally made her way back to the kitchen, the chill in her bones from the night air told her a cup of hot chocolate was in order because tea was not her…cup of tea. The kitchen wasn't large but was well stocked. It was set up in a straight line with the fridge on one side and the stove and sink on the other. White cabinets lined the walls floor to ceiling, broken up by the gray stone counter. At one end of the room was a closet-like pantry with a stout wooden door. At the other was an adjacent eating area with a round oak table surrounded by a bank of windows facing out to sea.

What a lovely place to start your day. Too bad the sun had set and the only light came from inside the house. Outside was pitch black.

Everything about the kitchen screamed homey. It was hard to believe anything as horrible as what Brian had claimed could have happened here. Sloane thought it was the perfect house and could see why Brian and his wife were so in love with the place. She was falling in love with the place, and she'd only been here a few hours.

Sloane rummaged through the cabinets next to the stove. If it was her house, that's where she'd keep hot chocolate. She found a pack of instant cocoa and a metal pot which she filled with milk from the fridge.

She'd set the pot on the trivet and the flame sputtered to life on the old gas stove when a slow chill crept down her spine. Maybe she wasn't as alone as she thought.

Grabbing a bottle of water out of the fridge, she twisted the cap, taking a long drink as she scanned the room.

All her senses screamed at her. Someone was watching but something felt off. It didn't feel like any entity she'd ever encountered before. Could it be a human? Goosebumps prickled her arms and a tingle of fear caught in her throat.

An old broom leaned against the wall next to the stove. Sloane reached for it, arming herself in case someone was there. If those ghost hunters were stalking her, she'd be ready. Whistling and pushing the broom to relax herself, she made a slow turn and scanned the room.

Nothing.

Turning back to the stove, a shadow flashed in her peripheral vision. Flipping the broom upside down, she pivoted around wielding her broom like a weapon. No shadows. Bright overhead bulbs lit the entire room, even that corner by the pantry. Could something be hiding in there? An old house might have mice or a rat or two, even with all the work that had been done.

Tiptoeing to the pantry door with her make-shift broom at the ready, she flung open the pantry door.

Nothing.

Shelves stocked in haphazard disarray with dusty canned goods. No signs of a rodent infestation.

I'm losing it. After returning the broom to its original spot, she turned back to the task at hand of waiting for her milk to bubble. She clutched her water bottle in her hand so tight it began to crinkle and fold in on itself. Loosening her grip, she drained the last few drops.

Every few minutes, she glanced over her shoulder, still not able to shake the feeling that something was there, moving in the shadowy corner. Being alone in any big house could be creepy. Sloane couldn't decide if the house itself was spooky or if she was letting her nerves get to her. The nagging knowledge she should stop taking these cases alone ate away at her psyche.

But taking a partner meant she had to admit Jonah was right. She hated doing that.

A shadow moved at the edge of her vision again, and Sloane turned. She faced the sink, gazing though the beveled glass, trying to see what was behind her.

She felt a tap on the shoulder.

"Sloane!"

Hearing her name sent her into overdrive, she grabbed the broom, spinning in one motion. She accidentally swung it around, flipping over the pot and spraying hot milk around the room like machine gun fire. Before Sloane could take a breath, the bristles of the broom were ablaze!

"Brian!" Sloane gasped. "What are you doing here?"

"I asked for you to find my wife, not burn the place down," Brian said.

"Shit!" Thinking fast, Sloane dunked the broom into the sink, flipping on the water. The flames hissed but went out, leaving a trail of smoke behind.

"What are you doing here?" she shrieked.

"The police brought me in for questioning but according to them, they didn't have enough evidence to hold me. Can you believe they actually think I did something to Rin?" Brian sat down at the kitchen table, leaning over to rub one hand over his head.

"You look horrible," Sloane said, going to sit beside him.

"Never one to mince your words, were you?" Brian asked. Sloane shrugged in response. "The police think I'm nuts. Now I'm starting to think I'm nuts. I tried to tell the police Rin isn't officially a missing person because she got sucked into a mirror. They actually had the audacity to ask if she might have left me and advised me to get psychiatric counseling! Can you believe that? She's pregnant with my child, but they won't listen to me."

Sloane looked away as Brian wiped his tears. She wasn't good with emotional outbursts from other people. She had enough of them herself.

"What exactly did you tell them?" she asked when she was sure he had control again.

"The truth," Brian insisted. "She was pulled into some kind of portal in the master bathroom's mirror."

"Why would they believe that?" Sloane snorted in disbelief.

"Because it's the truth," Brian insisted.

Sloane didn't need to point out to him that his "truth" was pretty unbelievable.

"What have you found out?" Brian asked. "Please tell me you found something."

"Oh, there's something in this house. That much I can tell you, but I don't know much more. I just got here. I need more time."

"I don't have time. I can't sneeze without the police asking me if I washed my hands. No one believes me, but at least they've agreed to keep this quiet because of Jonah's influence and my being a so-called celebrity. There isn't a body, so they can't prove I've done anything wrong, but that doesn't mean they can't make my life hell while they search for clues that aren't there. They think I've lost my mind. Maybe I have. I don't care. I just want my wife back."

"Why don't you talk me though what happened that night," Sloane suggested. "Slowly, one detail at a time."

"Ok." Brian stood, leading Sloane out of the kitchen and into the entry. "We had just gotten here. I went upstairs while Rin was putting out some stuff to make it smell nicer. I was looking at this when I felt something behind me." Brian pointed to some words in the wall. "I saw something move over my shoulder. It went into the bathroom. Then Rin came up and said she needed to use the bathroom. I didn't want her to go in there, but I thought I was being irrational. She started screaming. By the time the door opened, it was too late."

Sloane followed Brian into the bathroom. It looked the same as before, except this time the mirror looked like it had just been covered in a layer of steam.

"Did you shower in here?" Brian asked.

"No, the mirror shouldn't be fogged up like this."

A letter took shape, like a person was using their finger on the steam, but no one was touching the glass.

S

"What's going on here?" Sloane leaned closer, making sure she didn't touch the mirror.

L

"Whoa." Brian reached for the glass.

O

"Wait." Sloane leaned closer to the mirror. Her neck started to sting, as if something was clawing at her throat, but she couldn't take her eyes off the word forming to check what was there. She covered her neck with her hand, watching the next letter appear.

A

"Where's my wife?" he screamed at the mirror.

N

They backed out of the bathroom together as the last letter took shape.

E

"That's it." Brian pulled her down the stairs and toward the front door. "No way are you staying here. We need to call the police…and Jonah, and—"

Pulling her arm free from his vice-like grip, she had to scream to get him to shut up. "Brian! You have to calm down. This is what I do. You can leave, but I'm staying. You bought a haunted house. And if what you say is true, wherever Rin is, we need to get her back as soon as possible."

"You think she's alive?" His voice broke. "I just want her back. Safe."

The words coming from Sloane's mouth exuded more of a convincing tone than she felt. Her throat felt dry and her neck stung. She knew without looking there were scratches lining her throat. Hunching her shoulders, she tried to keep Brian from seeing them. She needed some water, but she'd left her bottle in the kitchen. Fear was pressing down on her. And Brian should not stay. His energy was negative to the point of violent.

Besides, she told herself, *I work best alone.*

Buttoning a jacket he'd left by the front door, Brian ignored her, setting Sloane's teeth on edge. "Sloane, am I nuts? I didn't think so a few days ago, but now…"

"We both saw the mirror,,, If someone or something is trying to harass me or a spirit is trying to tell me something, I won't leave until I know the truth."

They locked eyes for a moment. He didn't budge. "You have scratches on your neck that weren't there before. Don't try to hide it. That thing is out to get you. Are you really going to make me call Jonah to talk some sense into you?" Brian crossed his arms over his chest, looking down his nose at her. His intent was to intimidate. Luckily Sloane wasn't an easy target.

"Do whatever you want." She huffed. "By the way, so far I don't feel like there's anything evil in this house. I'm sure there's a spirit here, but I haven't been able to figure out why it's here. I'm not in any danger."

"I didn't think Rin and I were in danger either, and look what happened."

Sloane sighed. She wasn't going to be able to reason with him. It was his fear talking, maybe irrational, maybe not. And speaking of irrational fears, she pushed past him, headed into the kitchen, and picked up her discarded bottle. It was still half full. She sipped it this time, as she came back into the parlor, deciding what to do. He wouldn't back down. She knew it.

"Why call Jonah?" she asked. "You did request me, didn't you?"

"Jonah recommended you. Said you'd be the best one for the job," Brian said evasively. "But I didn't think it would target you too."

"It's not targeting. It may be asking…" She started, but he wasn't listening. He'd already pulled open the front door and was waiting for her in the threshold.

"We're leaving," he said. It was not so much a request as an order.

Chapter Four

"Hi, you've reached Jonah. Leave me a message. Unless you're the delivery guy and can't find me. Then hit eight and you'll be connected to the desk who will track me down immediately as I am probably damn hungry by now ... beeeeep."

Sloane snorted. "Nice message, dork. I'm here. Kind of safe and sound for the moment but with some issues. Brian's story is checking out." She gave Brian a thumbs up as they descended the front steps and began pacing in front of the house She lowered her voice. "I'm pretty sure we're dealing with a shadow person and a nasty one who might have found a portal and literally dragged Rin through it. When you have a sec, call me back. I need a little advice. Only advice. Not you, on the next flight here or anything..." she paused, thinking of how nice that would be, "...but sooner than later on that call so I can run my game plan past you. I don't want to screw anything up and lose Rin. By the way, for what it's worth, I miss you." Those last three words, she'd whispered.

He was probably on a jog with his blonde bombshell partner and then busting the world's worst notorious criminals without breaking a sweat. No, that wasn't true. Lately he'd been working a lot more than usual. He used to work solely in the paranormal division, but lately she'd begun to suspect he was working on different cases. *Get it together! Count on no one but yourself. Jonah can't always be around to help you!*

She filtered through her knowledge of shadow people: they're all different, not all bad. They commonly appear in mirrors with red or yellow eyes. Some are demonic.

"Get in my car. I need food. And I'm not going back inside that place. Neither are you until we hear back from Jonah. Brian drove to a twenty-four-hour diner, where he ordered a chicken-fried steak and eggs, and Sloane sipped stale black coffee and poked at a cinnamon bun. How he could eat was beyond her. Halfway through the meal, both their phones dinged with incoming texts:

Jonah: *I'm sending reinforcements. Stay out of the house for now.*

"Whatever," Sloane said to no one, disgruntled. What reinforcements would he send? The local sheriff? Some retired FBI contact? Rin was in danger, there was no time to waste.

"Good," Brian said, wiping his stubble with a napkin. You stay in a hotel until Jonah gives us more instructions. I'll drop you off at the house. Get your stuff and get a hotel room. Agreed?"

"That does sound like the best course of action for now," Sloane lied. No way was she leaving that house. Even though every time she was inside the place, it seemed like her mind found a good reason for her to leave, but once she was outside, she couldn't remember why she had left. It was like the place wanted her there as much as it was trying to force her to leave.

"I'll wait for you here," Brian said when they

43

pulled back up to the house.

"It's really not necessary. I have to turn off my equipment, and I'll be on my way. Call me tomorrow?" She gave her sweetest "I'm doing-what-I'm-told" smile.

"Promise? Because this place gives me the creeps. And I need to shower and shave something fierce. Jonah will know what to do."

It took every fiber of her being not to roll her eyes. Of course, the almighty Jonah, to the rescue. Again. "I'm right behind you."

She watched him pull out of the driveway, pebbles crackling under the tires. She wasn't sure she wanted to stay. But couldn't bring herself to leave, either. So she made a detour to the beach. Small bonfire pits were ablaze in both directions. The cool, evening surf called out to her. Slipping off her shoes, she waded barefoot into the waves. The ocean lapped at her ankles, and the moon cast long silver shadows on the undulating water.

So much water. Salt water. Not the same. Nothing to drink.

And people died in the ocean every day. In the circle of life, violent bloody feeding on one another dominated. Was that the answer? In everything beautiful there was also evil and darkness?

The moon, round and chubby in the night sky, gave her an answer. In the darkness, there was light. Inhaling, she found her own balance, her own personal place in the universe for this moment.

The wind whipped her hair around her. In this moment of transcendental repose, she threw her head back and laughed. "Ha! I get it now." She spoke to no one. As usual.

What was going on here? Why wasn't she inside the house monitoring her equipment? This whole *laissez-faire* attitude was not like her. Almost like…she turned to stare at the house.

The house was playing with her. Putting her at ease. Distracting her from the real job.

Find Rin. Save Rin.

Every moment she was gone, there was a slimmer chance she could return. Sloane listened to the rustle of the wind on the beach and the roar of the surf. The old house seemed to call out to her. Like it missed her being there. And how could she disappoint it?

But this time, she would protect herself before going inside.

This wasn't something she'd learned in therapy, but something Jonah had taught her. It was like meditation, but there was more to it. It was a way to not only gather herself, but to protect her soul.

The nurturing, stable earth underfoot fed her desire for permanence in her impermanent life. The light from the strong-willed fires up and down the beach fed her need for energy. The breath of life wind whipped her dark hair around her face where she willed good energy inward and negative energy to be carried out to sea. Lastly, she allowed the cooling effects of the water to hydrate her through cleansing and purification.

Warmth spread throughout her whole body quenching a thirst where water could never reach. The world tilted back into balance. The wind and waves soothed like a gentle lullaby as opposed to a harsh clattering of mayhem and racket. Above, the moon shone more silver. Sloane's heart lightened.

She glanced back at the house and felt as if it was

watching her. Judging her with its glass windows and painted shutters.

All at once, her mind snapped back to reality.

There was *something* to what she'd just experienced embracing the elements. *But what?* A spirituality of sorts she'd connected to. Popping her trunk to grab her equipment bags, she found a lump in one of the pockets. Unzipping the bag, she found a small brown paper bag wrapped with twine nestled among her equipment. Inside were a cloth bag with few shiny stones and a small plastic vial of liquid with a black screw-on lid marked with Jonah's writing.

She shook it and read the bottle:

> *Purify, cleanse, and protect*
> *From what's not in sight.*
> *Bathe me and my spirit*
> *In universal light.*

Damn, that awesome jackass. Jonah. Around even when he wasn't around. Her phone dinged with an incoming text. *"Knowing you, you're still there. Alone. If your stubbornness does not allow you listen to my sound advice, at least protect yourself. Last time I saw you, I left something in with your equipment. In a paper bag. Say the words and put some behind your neck and on your wrists. I had my aunt make it just for you, and yes, she's on her way. Put the stones in your pocket. Be safe and stay in touch."*

Jonah's aunt was a famous East Coast psychic. Good grief. When he said he was calling in reinforcements, he wasn't kidding. The woman was a legend. Working with her would be amazing.

A second text came through a few seconds later, *"PS, I miss you, too."*

Slone felt a warmth form deep in her chest. She may not need him around, but it was good to know he was always there.

After saying the words and dabbing the liquid as instructed, she checked her three static night vision cameras—the thermal one aimed at the corner of the kitchen where she'd glimpsed the shadow. The other two, she set on night vision—one in the upstairs hallway and the other in the parlor. She rewound the tapes.

Zilch. No new evidence.

Her brand new Ghost Box Ovilus V had fresh batteries, and her handheld EVP recorder hung around her neck. The Ovilus could convert environmental readings into words. Spirits could alter electromagnetic frequencies or temperatures to allow an intelligent entity to "speak." It had set her back close to three-hundred dollars with shipping, and she prayed the Ovilus would help her understand what she was up against.

The nerve center was up and running in the kitchen, recording everything. For now, she'd avoid the bathroom, but now was the time to see who or what was here and if it was willing to show itself. Her stomach had decided to rebel against her not having more to eat at the diner and growled with fury.

Pizza and company. Her heart ached for her old ghost hunting days. She and Jonah always ordered pizza to be delivered to scare the crap out of the rest of their team when the doorbell rang. They'd giggle and nibble on pepperoni and olive pizza together in darkened hallways. It was no wonder she hadn't made contact until she stopped working with him.

The memory tugged at her. After the Glen and Alvin case, she knew she needed a partner. But the idea of alerting local paranormal teams to her investigations wasn't appealing to her. She needed someone green. Someone she could train from the ground up.

So that left her with…no one.

A little voice told her to leave. Order a pizza. Go to the hotel. She decided to test out her theory. This was the house, begging for her not to delve into its secrets, but sad every time she left. "I wish I could do this, but I should wait until tomorrow night. Being here alone is flat-out stupidity." She said to no one, hoping the house would hear her and think it won.

Again.

The second she stepped outside, the feeling passed. It *was* the house messing with her! Apparently Jonah's words and potion at least let her break past its basic spell. The night air once again calmed her, and she drew the beauty of the place around her. The pristine ocean sang with rhythmic waves while bending to the moon's whims.

She sat on the front porch, trying to decide what to do. Her gut said to leave, but once she was outside the house, she immediately felt the pull to go back inside. She'd have to buy Brian and Rin a Ying-Yang to hang inside this place.

Headlights slowed from the south and pulled into the driveway. Great, Brian had come back to yell at her for still being here. She crossed her arms and waited. It better not be those twin pop tarts. She'd already had enough of them for one day.

The car jolted into park and the engine got quiet. The girl, the nice one, got out of her car—*alone*—

carrying Sloane's heart's desire.

A square cardboard box.

Sloane bounded up to her, actually happy to have the company of the one person who didn't completely annoy her today. But what was the girl's name again? She wracked her brain. "Hi, you're back?"

"Sorry to show up so late and I know you didn't want our help, but I thought you might be hungry. And I really wanted to hear how you are doing, because I'm pretty sure the rest of my team are frauds."

"Hungry? It's eleven o'clock." Sloane took the pizza and peeked inside. Straight up pepperoni. The girl could stay. "It's pizza. Of course I'm hungry. Where's your friend? Tall, gangly guy with glasses?"

"Kevin's not here. Just me, this time. I hope that's ok?" She shifted from one foot to the other, betraying her insecurity.

"I can pay for the pizza, and honestly, I'm happy to see you. But I'm sorry, I forgot your name."

"It's Whitney. Are you sure you don't mind me here? I know I don't have the written authorization you were talking about…" She lingered by her car as if waiting for a real invitation.

"Of course I don't. The written contract also says that I can bring in any help I desire as part of my investigation. Why do you say your team is a bunch of frauds?" Sloane's sneakers creaked on the whiteboard steps. She plopped down in a rocking chair resting the pizza box on the wide banister. She dug out the biggest piece and bit down on the warm, gooey deliciousness.

"Kevin's not," she was quick to say. "The Besses are wannabes, and Hank only does what he's told. But I don't have anyone else to teach me how to use my gift."

"Uh-huh," Sloane mumbled still chewing her pizza. She swallowed and looked—really looked—at the girl. A slight tremor held both the girl's hands captive, and her foot shook with a nervous twitch reflex. Whitney's blue eyes reflected one thing: terrified naivety.

Poor thing.

Pausing in her attempt to devour another slice of heaven, she put a hand on Whitney's knee. "You've seen things?"

The girl nodded. "All my life," she breathed.

Sloane sensed the girl didn't want to talk about it, and she wasn't one to pry. Everyone had their own hang-ups. She was practically a vampire because of her delayed sleep phase disorder—which she was working on—and her irrational fear of dehydration. Well, maybe it wasn't irrational considering what happened, but it felt irrational. There was no term for her phobia. She was considering coining the phrase 'dehydrophobia.' It sounded legit.

"I wish you and I were on the couch of my apartment, eating pizza and drinking wine. You know…having a girls' night in." Whitney had changed the subject, but Sloane didn't mind. The thin red-head grabbed another slice of pizza from the box, taking a huge bite.

Sloane laughed. She couldn't remember the last time she'd had a girls' night in. She had a sudden impulse and went with it.

"Well, maybe someday, Whitney," Sloane hedged. "But tonight, we're at an abandoned home where I need to figure out what is here and if it really is dangerous for the new owners. My equipment is recording as we speak. So, are you in?"

Whitney's eyes were wide. "Really? Are you sure?"

Sloane took a bite of pizza to stall for a moment before she responded, thinking she'd feel the same regret she always felt when she tried to find someone to work with. But it didn't happen. She actually felt kind of excited about it.

"Let's start in the kitchen," she suggested. "I kept seeing shadows at the edge of my vision. Let's go see if something doesn't want us here. We need to call it out, talk to it, and get it to appear and answer our questions."

"Is that where you got those scratches on your neck?" Whitney pointed, fishing a small mirror out of her purse.

Sloane examined her neck. The scratches were deeper than she thought. Almost actual cuts. "I guess so. Not sure what made them though." Before they went inside, she explained how the house would try to get her to leave and gave Whitney the words of protection and dabbed the liquid on her neck and wrists. "Now you're ready. Buckle up, kiddo."

They packed up the pizza and made their way to the kitchen nerve center where they found the thermal camera upside down on the floor. "Crap, how did that fall?" Sloane rushed to pick it up and make sure it wasn't broken. Then she reset the camera more securely on its tripod.

Whitney gave her a hand securing the tripod. "I was serious about the wine and pizza girls'-night-in idea. Sometimes being normal would be nice."

"I hear you, but I have to admit, I like being me

most of the time, and I'm anything but normal," Sloane replied.

"Nice nerve center. May I?" Whitney asked.

"Yeah. Let's go ahead and rewind and watch the footage. I want to know what happened to this camera." Sloane went to work on the computer. All at once, something on the footage caught her eye. Something the thermal camera caught before it fell.

Whitney was fiddling around with the other equipment. "Is this an Ovilus? I've heard about these. The spirits can channel their energy and form words that come through here, right? It's like having a conversation with them. I'm going to go outside and get the cheap one I carry in my car and—"

Sloane held up a finger. "Stay here. I am starting to see that every time I start to investigate I find some crazy reason to go outside or get distracted. This house has secrets it doesn't want to share. Fight the impulse to leave and keep your feet planted right where they are." Sloane went to rewind the thermal camera and watched the recorded footage again. "Whoa, Whitney. You have to see this!"

Whitney moved to behind the monitor, and Sloane replayed the thermal recording again. In the last frame before the camera went to static, something with a heat signature—all reds and oranges—rushed the camera. Sloane rewound it again and again. "Are those…?" She paused it and cocked her head.

"Fingers?" Whitney suggested. "Hard to say if that's a person or not. Can I turn on the Ovilus?"

"Ok." Sloane focused on the computer playing and replaying the footage and pausing it at different intervals hoping to find something concrete.

"LEAVE." A computer-generated voice said through her new Ovilus V.

Sloane whipped around and looked at Whitney. who she clutched the device to her chest. Sloane knew that look. It was the look of someone who wasn't used to this. The voice wasn't from a benevolent spirit but something much more sinister. And it wanted them to leave.

"Why should we leave?" Sloane asked.

Two words spoken in rapid succession on the Ovilus made them both freeze in their tracks.

"You're…"

"Next."

Chapter Five

"*Who's* next?" Sloane asked.

There was no answer.

Whitney grabbed onto Sloane's arm, her excitement evident.

"Come on. That's not fair," Whitney was breathless. "You can't leave us hanging like this."

Although trying to appear calm herself, Sloane knew how she felt. It was the same for her after every other-worldly encounter.

The Ovilus was silent. The presence—whatever it was—was gone.

"I'm getting more than I bargained for in this house." Sloane grabbed the Ovilus, tucked it into the camera bag she'd bought for it, and threw the cord around her neck. The thing was expensive, and she didn't want to inadvertently drop and break it. "Come on, I'll show you around."

"So you're going to let me stay?" Whitney asked.

"You just had an encounter with a presence and you didn't even flinch," Sloane said. "You either have nerves of steel, or you were made for this job. Plus, it threatened us. There's power in numbers even though I hate to admit it. Plus, you brought me pizza. You're on my A-list for that."

"I promise I won't be any trouble," Whitney hurried to say. "I'll stay out of your way, do whatever you ask me to and…"

"For now let's walk the house." They left the camera running in the kitchen. There was a chance whatever was attached to the hand in the video would return.

The kitchen was the only room in the house with renovations. The rest of the house looked like it had come straight out of the turn of the nineteenth century. It was beautiful, though parts of it were desperately in need of restoration.

The main living area was a long rectangular room with a distinctively Victorian look. There was scalloped crown molding along the ceiling and long moth-eaten green velvet curtains on the large bay windows.

A fireplace graced one end of the room but was so blackened and dirty it would be dangerous to light a fire. In front of the hearth were two walnut and button style balloon backed chairs, upholstered with a hideous yellow fabric.

The dining room had etched tin ceilings, faded with age, but would have been elegance personified when the house was built. Now the oak table was covered in a thick layer of dust.

The first thing she'd recommend to Brian was a cleaning crew. The kitchen was great—and full of food—but the rest of the house needed work.

But he'd done the right thing. If they'd disturbed a spirit by being in the house, it was best to leave everything alone until the ghost had been dealt with by a professional.

As Sloane led Whitney up the elegant mahogany staircase lined with a tattered green floral runner, she got an idea.

"Hey, have you lived here long?" she asked.

"Pretty much my whole life." Whitney ran one finger over the dust on an oval portrait in the hall revealing a young man with a curled handlebar moustache. It was one of many lining the landing at the top of the stairs.

"Do you know why this house has been empty for so long?" Sloane asked.

"I know the rumors, which might not be the truth," Whitney said.

"Sometimes there are flickers of truth in rumors."

Whitney peeked into a bedroom. It was the one Sloane had decided to call the military room, with American Civil War portraits and a pair of crossed cavalry swords on the wall. There were two more bedrooms on the second floor. One a floral disaster with a dusty canopy bed. The other was a small room that might have been for a child. That was the one Sloane had chosen for herself.

"Well, one rumor is that the owner moved to Europe and kept the house for tax reasons," Whitney said.

Sloane couldn't help her expression of disbelief.

"I know. Too boring. I have more." Whitney laughed. "Is this the master suite?" She opened the door at the end of the hall.

"No, that's the stairway up to the widow's walk; the master suite is over here."

"Oh, I see." Whitney shivered, closing the door. "That goes well with the second rumor."

"What's that?" Sloane asked.

"They say the woman who lived here had a husband and a son who were both lost at sea. She never recovered from the loss. Her spirit still walks the house in a flowing white dress, standing on the widow's walk every night to wait for her loved ones to come home."

"A flowing white dress?" Sloane scoffed. "That's the oldest story in the ghost haunting book. Why is it female ghosts always wear white? I'd love to see one wear a nice blue dress."

"I know." Whitney laughed. "I didn't make up the rumors."

"Anything else?" Sloane opened the door to the master suite and ushered Whitney inside.

"The last one is the best," Whitney said. "They say the woman who used to live here was a sensitive, but she went completely insane. She was obsessed with talking to the dead. They say she wanted revenge, but no one knows who she was trying to curse. She held some kind of séance here and opened a portal to hell."

"Oooo, that is a good one." Sloane laughed. "And it kind of makes sense. It would explain some of the things happening here."

Whitney walked to the sink, leaning close to check her reflection in the mirror. Sloane caught her breath; for a moment she swore Whitney's reflection changed. Instead of a petite red head, a brown-haired beauty pounded on the glass, a dark shadow looming behind her. Whitney stumbled back away from the mirror, tripping over her feet and banging into the wall as the image disappeared.

"Who was that?" Whitney rubbed her bare arms with her hands, her breath coming out as a fog.

"Rin?" Sloane stepped toward the mirror. Little frost-like crystals were forming on the glass, making a silvery frame around her image. She didn't need her digital thermometer to tell her the temperature in the room had just dropped significantly.

Whitney edged in next to her, and they both stared into the mirror, waiting. Something was here with them, but what?

Sloane stared at her own reflection, and her vision tunneled until nothing else seemed to exist, darkness surrounding her like a shroud. She watched her face in the mirror morph into something sinister, but still a version of herself. Her cheeks hollowed out as her pupils dilated to cover the whites of her eyes. Her hair fell out in clumps, leaving a corpse-like image staring back at her. She couldn't look away. Gripping the countertop with both hands, she tilted her head to the side and the image followed. She recognized it as a piece of her, everything she hated about herself stared back at her. Her grief. Pain. Longing. And yet she felt oddly comfortable in its presence.

A hand rose from beneath the frame inside the mirror, a long sharp nail protruding from the thumb. The emaciated reflection of her face grimaced at her as the sharpened thumbnail traced a line across her neck from one ear to the other in a universal symbol for death. Sloane watched, entranced, as the blood dripped down her throat, funneling into the hollow between her breasts.

Whitney's scream broke whatever spell had been on her, and Sloane jerked back, only her two-handed grip on the counter keeping her from falling. She blinked, and her vision returned to normal, the darkness retreating. She could once again see her normal self in the mirror with Whitney's pale face reflected beside her. They each had a thin red line across their throats as if they'd been scratched.

"What was that?" Whitney asked, her hands clutching her neck. "It was me, but I looked dead!"

Sloane took a deep breath, trying to radiate calm. Whitney's excited state would not help their investigation.

"There's an entity inside that mirror!" Whitney ran toward the door. "I have to go get my camera!"

"Your camera? What are you talking about?" Sloane couldn't understand the girl's train of thought.

"I need to get a picture of what's going on here. This is amazing. I'll be right back."

"Wait, no, Whitney, stay here." Sloane reached for her arm, but Whitney sped out of the room and the door slammed closed behind her. The lights flicked, and then went out.

Without windows, the small bathroom was completely dark. Sloane felt her way to the door, bumping past the toilet and stubbing her toe into a wall. She found the light switch and flipped it on. Nothing happened.

Groping around, she found the door handle and tried the knob. It wouldn't turn.

"Whitney, this isn't funny." Sloane pounded one fist on the door. "I'm seriously rethinking this whole working together thing."

There wasn't an answer. If anything, the darkness deepened. Sloane felt her way along the wall, back to the sink. Maybe she could turn on the tap and try to scoop some water into her dry throat. But she couldn't find the sink.

She kept her hand on the wall, using it as a guide. But it never ended. She turned, trying to find the door, but it had disappeared as well. It was like she was trapped in a circular room with no doors and no windows.

Or a circular pit like the one she'd been trapped in before. She had a sudden image of Glen, the sick pervert who'd trapped her in a pit and waited around to watch her die. She'd never felt more helpless, knowing she was one in a line of girls he'd trapped to kill for fun.

Her breath started to come in short gasps. She tried to calm herself but felt the panic rising. Putting her back to the wall, she sank down until she was sitting on the cold stone floor. Trapped. And she hated being trapped. Almost as much as she hated being thirsty.

She put her head between her knees, closing her eyes and taking deep breaths.

"You are not in that pit. This isn't real," she told herself over and over. "This is a bathroom, and you'll find your way out."

"Hello. Is someone there?"

Sloane stilled. She didn't know that voice. Was there someone else in the room?

"Can anyone hear me?"

Picking up her head, Sloane saw Rin on the wrong side of the mirror. Her hands were up, palms facing out, and Sloane realized they were flattened, as if she was leaning against a glass wall. "I can hear you." Sloane stood, moving to stand in front of the girl. "Rin?"

"Yes! Yes! It's Rin. Who's there?"

Sloane realized Rin couldn't see her. She could only hear her.

"It's Sloane. Jonah's old friend."

"Get me out of here!" Rin screamed. "It's coming!

It's coming! You have to help me!"

Rin started sobbing, as hands wrapped around her from behind. Though she fought, she was pulled screaming back into the abyss.

The light flicked on, and Sloane launched herself at the mirror, pushing on the glass. She wanted to pound on the glass but was afraid to break the mirror and lose Rin forever.

"Bring her back!" she yelled. "Do you hear me? Bring her back! You can't keep her in there. I'm going to get her out of there! Wherever you're keeping her, I'm going to find her!"

The bathroom door creaked open to a different world than the one she'd come from. It was the same room, but everything from the clean coat of paint on the walls to the duvet cover on the bed looked brand new. Daylight shone through the window, gleaming off the polished oak furniture.

Sloane blinked in denial. What was going on? How was this even possible?

She heard a soft sound, like a woman crying. Sloane followed the noise out of the master suite and down the hall. An open door led to the same room Sloane had chosen for herself when she arrived. It was the smallest bedroom, tucked in the corner between the master suite and the winding stairway to the widow's walk.

When Sloane reached the doorway, she saw the room was the same, but everything was like new. The chipped white iron bed stood in the same corner with a waterfall dresser across from it. A woman in a long blue skirt and a high collared white dress shirt crouched on the floor. Her long brown hair was in disarray and she clutched a pillow to her face as she sobbed.

"Hello," Sloane said. "Are you all right?"

The woman didn't respond, so Sloane stepped into the room and dropped to the floor beside the woman.

"Hello," she said again. "Can I help you? Why are you crying?"

She went to put her arm around the woman, but her arm passed right through as if no one was there.

Sloane fell back onto her bottom in shock.

What was happening here? None of this was possible.

The light faded and a shadow hovered over the woman, wrapping arms of darkness around her.

"Hey! What are you doing? Leave her alone!"

The shadow turned toward Sloane, glowing red eyes fixated on her, and Sloane froze. Literally. She couldn't move. It felt like ice encased her body from head to toe.

It hissed through pointed yellow teeth. Unwinding itself from around the crying woman, the shadow slithered along the floor like a snake, coming toward Sloane. Darkness oozed from the creature, as if it was made of shadows. The closer it got to Sloane, the more she could feel the hatred flowing from it.

She backed up, hit a wall, and the shadow was on top of her. She closed her eyes, feeling its cold breath in her face. She was going to die. She knew it. This thing was going to kill her, and then she wouldn't be able to save Rin.

Not too long ago she would have welcomed death because it would have reunited her with her fiancé, Michael.

But this time when she closed her eyes, all she

could see was Jonah's face. She loved the way his smile was just a little bit crooked. Thinking of him made her fear ease, and she waited for the phantom snake-like thing to strike.

But nothing happened.

Sloane cracked one eye open and realized she was crouched in the corner of the bathroom.

The door swung open, and Whitney stepped into the room, holding the camera in her hand.

"What are you doing?" Whitney asked, casually flipping on the lights.

"I was trapped," Sloane gasped. "How long was I gone? I couldn't get out. It locked me in here. I saw Rin and the house as it was years ago. I walked through it. The shadow person came at me. It was horrible. I can't… I don't…"

"Sloane." Whitney's voice was calm and even. She put down the camera and placed a hand on Sloane's arm. "What are you talking about? I literally left you a minute ago."

Chapter Six

After Sloane explained what had happened in the bathroom, Whitney suggested they take a break outside. The smart girl grabbed the leftover pizza off the kitchen counter before leading the shaken Sloane outside. The cool sand squeaked between their toes. They sat side by side on the beach, tilting the cardboard lid to block the wind from blowing sand onto the pizza. They stared at the waning crescent moon, and Sloane took a deep, breath of the fresh, night air, preparing herself to push the younger girl a bit, to see how she was handling all of this.

"Whitney, I know I let it go before, but can I ask you a question now?"

The girl stopped turned her full attention to Sloane. "Sure."

"I know you didn't want to answer before, but I think I'd like to know now. Why are you doing this?"

Whitney's expression grew distant and she took a moment before speaking. "I don't know about you, but for me, it's dumb, really. I lost someone, and I want concrete evidence that there's something after this life."

Sloane sniffed. "I understand more than you think. I lost my fiancé."

Whitney covered Sloane's hand with her own. "Your fiancé? Wow, I'm so sorry. That's awful. What happened?"

Good listeners were a dying breed. Sloane counted the good listeners she knew on one hand: Jonah and…well, maybe that was it. Jonah and now Whitney. Or maybe it was the fact she never allowed herself to get close enough to anyone anymore. You can't share your intimate emotions with total strangers. And most of the people Sloane met were so self-absorbed that after she shared something, they always managed to turn the conversation back around to themselves.

"Car accident. But want to know something? At one house I investigated, I *saw* him. Helped him move on even." She twisted the engagement ring still on her finger. "One of these days, I guess I'll have to do the same."

"Holy shit, Sloane. That's incredible."

Empathy. Whitney made her feel like someone else gave a shit. A shoulder to lean on.

"Sometimes you can't move on. No matter how hard you try," Whitney said.

The girl spoke from some kind of personal experience of her own. "Want to talk about it?" Sloane hadn't had a girlfriend in so long. Michael and his life were her life. And being alone and answering to no one was easier than faking small talk with the masses.

"My older sister and I shared a room. She had bad asthma and died of pneumonia as a teenager. I used to catch glimpses of her combing her hair in our bedroom. She was probably trying to tell me she was okay, but it scared me to death and I hated it. Now I see things out of the corner of my eye all the time. Like she opened some kind of gateway inside of me. For a while I thought I was crazy. Then I met Kevin. He's the only person who has ever understood me." A faint smile whispered at the corners of her mouth.

Sloane kept quiet, knowing there was more to the story.

"Even though I stopped seeing my sister when I hit my teens, I have never really let her go. I missed all these years of having my big sister around. Honestly, even if this sounds crazy, I've felt closer to you in one day than I have to anyone in a long while. I don't know. I just feel like you understand me and don't judge, if that makes sense. It probably doesn't, but that's how I feel."

Sloane draped her arm around the girl, and they munched on pizza and listened to the waves. "What do you say we call it a night? I'm exhausted. I think we have more than enough evidence of a legitimate haunting. Why don't you head home and give me a call tomorrow?"

"But I can load and reply and magnify all the EVPs and see what else we caught tonight. And go through the camera footage, and—"

"Tomorrow," Sloane insisted, closing the pizza box and brushing the sand off her shorts. "I need some sleep and seeing as I'm usually not a nocturnal sleeper, saying I'm tired is pretty significant seeing as daylight isn't coming for a few more hours." Once they were back inside, Sloane went room to room and turned off the cameras and the laptops.

"You're not seriously *staying* here alone, are you? Not after what's happened tonight?"

Sloane nodded without turning around. "Whatever is here showed us what it wanted us to see tonight. It might keep trying to make me leave, but it won't get what it wants. I need some sleep."

"I'll stay, too. I'll text Kevin. Even though we are not officially 'together'"—she made quotations marks with her fingers—"I promised I'd tell him what happened tonight."

Sloane laughed, wagging a finger at her. "I thought there was something going on between you two. I'm surprised he didn't come with you tonight to deliver the pizza."

"It's pretty new right now, but he's a good guy."

Sloane walked to the front door and opened it. "Scram, Whitney. Go home to your boyfriend. I'll get some sleep, and I promise you can come back tomorrow."

Without a word, Whitney jerked forward and gave Sloane a quick hug. "Sorry, I'm a hugger." Her new friend laughed. "You'll get used to it. This was the best night of ghost hunting I've ever had thanks to you. Goodnight, Sloane. I'll see you tomorrow."

What could she do but smile? Whitney turned what was always an uncomfortable moment for her—hugging a relative stranger—into fun. "I had a good time, too. It was nice to have company. I'll work on getting used to the hugging thing." Sloane locked the door and turned off the lights. *Damn, I hope I can sleep.* How many nights had she been tired and gone to bed only to stare at the ceiling until day broke? But with all the packing, flying, and driving, she'd been awake nearly two days and knew sleep had to be on the menu or going crazy would be dessert.

A huge coffee table volume on *Wines of the World* Sloane found in the kitchen made a nice doorstop in the other upstairs bathroom. She wasn't taking any chances. The book propped the door open while she brushed her teeth and got ready for bed. She should probably get a hotel room, but she was too stubborn. Leaving this house would be admitting she was afraid and nothing scared Sloane Osborne.

Or at least nothing she'd admit to.

She pulled out her own blanket and pillow and curled up in the small bedroom listening to the house. A clock ticked from some other room. Creaks and moans from the old house she debunked as reactions to the unrelenting Atlantic wind. "I'm going to sleep," she announced to the house and its ethereal tenants. "Leave me alone for a few hours."

After downing a room temperature bottle of water, she allowed any fear she had that the house might keep her awake to dissolve. She rolled over and for the first time in a long time, fell asleep immediately.

The dream was more of a vision. Something real, but I can't tell if it's past or future.

I am privy to a horror befalling.

The boat cracked and wheezed as it fought to remain upright against the slapping booms of the unrelenting roar of the waves. Salty air clogged my mouth and nose as the vessel lurched to and fro throwing my stomach into my mouth. Two men worked tirelessly pulling in their fishing lines and tying down everything they could.

Hanging onto the railing, the contents of my stomach projected over the side into the sea—the sea that seems miles beneath me. In the next second, a wall of water washed over us, choking the vessel inside its icy palm before releasing us for its next onslaught. The ship is like a lonely bobber in choppy water. The heavy, sheets of rain push in around me, making me claustrophobic in an endless sea. We are helpless, at the mercy of the deep blue sea. Choppy waves surge and roar before crashing over the deck. The captain can't hold her steady. We are lurched and jarred at the sea's whim with zero control over our fate.

We taste only the salty waters of doom.

My death.

Their death.

But who are they?

The two men yell orders back and forth to save the ship. The old captain with a wrinkled face pulls his way back to the helm to steer, his rubber boots sliding on the deck and his black, vinyl coat unable to ward off the rain. The younger one is determined to make it to the end of the boat. To do what? The old man yells and shakes his head.

"Let it go!"

But the boy wraps his fingers around the railing and pulls himself farther toward the bow. The next wave is massive. The boy's fingers slip. The boat tilts to its side.

Then he is gone. Washed away in blackness. Swallowed whole by an indifferent fluid fiend.

The old man howls, letting go of the wheel to untie and throw a circular life preserver over the side. He swipes at his face to clear his vision of rain. Or maybe tears. I can feel his sharp pain. He knows the boy is gone.

Sinking.

Sinking.

Water rolls in and consumes us.

No more hatches to batten down.

All is lost.

He cast me one long look...before we sink.

"Sloane...Sloane." Flora perched in the doorway of Sloane's bedroom, still dressed in her tea-length blue dress. It looked sort of vintage, and Sloane wondered if it was something she'd found in the attic, or—more likely—made herself. "Wake up, sleepyhead, there's breakfast downstairs."

Immediately aware of her arms flailing around like a lunatic, Sloane pretended instead to stretch rather than swim. "Good morning Flora. Sorry, I'm kind of a night owl, but what are you doing here anyway?"

"Oh, this and that. Sorry to be so nosy, but I'm dying to know, how did it go last night? Find anything horrifying?"

Seeing as Flora wasn't really her client, Sloane felt like she'd be breaching client confidentiality if she told Rin's neighbor about last night. And would she even believe her?

"It went as well as can be expected for a first night. I'm still gathering evidence. I need more, maybe two more nights to get some answers."

"Well, hurry up. I miss Rin and Brian. Good kids, those two."

Sloane agreed and pulled on a sweatshirt and socks and padded downstairs after Flora.

"You said many generations of fishermen lived in this house?" Sloane asked, changing the subject.

"That's right." She pointed at the kitchen island. "Somebody likes you. They brought fresh muffins and a thermos of coffee."

"Whitney must have. The girl seems to like feeding me. Weird though. I thought I locked the door last night. I'll have to be better about that in the future. Of course, if it means muffins in the morning, maybe not." Sloane bit into a still warm chocolate chip muffin and poured some powdered creamer from the cupboard into a mug from the cabinet. "Were any of the men who lived in this house lost at sea? I had a really weird dream last night."

"Probably too many to count. It's an old house. But you can check at the historical center downtown. I'm sure they would be public record." Flora retied her belt and smoothed the front of her raincoat. "And I unlocked the door this morning. If I had my way there would be no locked doors in Yarmouth, sweetie. Now, if you don't need anything else, I have a few errands to run today."

Sloane gave her a warm smile. "I really appreciate you checking in on me. But I'm doing fine here and I'm used to being on my own."

Flora gave her a motherly look of concern. "Everyone needs family. I'm expecting mine home any time now, and I'm going to cook them a big welcome home dinner. Maybe we can all eat together?"

"I'd like that." Sloane grabbed her purse. "I think I am going to run into town to see what information I can find. Can you lock up?"

"No problem," Flora called after her.

Main Street in Yarmouth was a whole two blocks long and consisted of a town square that neatly housed a library, bank, hair salon, family grocery store, and coffee house around a square plot of grass, and a covered pavilion set up for summer concerts and farmers' markets. Sloane had no trouble easing into a parking spot a few steps from the library's front door.

Yarmouth embodied warmth and welcome, with

none of the usual frenzy of the east coast. This seaside town catered to neither tourists nor business people. The relaxed pace reminded her of lazy Midwest farm towns where last names were worn like a badge of honor showing the multiple generations continuing down their ancestors' chosen path. In the Midwest, that meant farming. Here, it meant fishing.

The seven rough stone steps to the refurbished stone mansion that was now the library had a pounded metal sign by the night book drop indicating it was 'Built in 1878' and was on the registry of 'Historic Places'.

Pushing past the double doors, Sloane glanced at multiple flyers tacked to a corkboard about youth movie night, children's reading hour, and local book clubs.

Michael had spent hours in medical libraries studying for exams and memorizing the names and connections between bones, muscles, and tendons. Sloane hadn't been one for studying. She'd rather be out in the field, learning as she went. The last time she'd been in a library had been with him. While Michael poured over thick verbose books with the human body diagrammed and dissected, Sloane had read cheesy romance novels with a guaranteed "happily ever after."

Never again.

Nothing was guaranteed.

With no other neighbors to interview and Brian not answering his cell phone, at least this library was cozy and small-town, not like the massive university libraries she and Michael used to frequent.

The main circulation desk housed two librarians who stood side by side sorting returned books in dead silence. The woman was at least thirty years Sloane's senior with blue tinged gray hair curled to perfection. Sloane was sure she had a weekly appointment at the hair salon down the street and showered with one of those fancy caps from the fifties. Her counterpart was a potbellied man who was twenty years older than the woman. She couldn't imagine he wasn't retired. Maybe volunteering in his golden years to keep his mind sharp?

A few scattered patrons sat at sturdy wooden tables perusing periodicals and paperbacks. The early bird in these small towns must get the best books. The doors couldn't have been unlocked for more than ten minutes.

The musty smell of old paper, the whisper of pages turning, and hushed murmurs reminded Sloane to be on her best behavior.

Not one of her strong suits.

Sloane approached the female librarian hoping her computer skills outweighed that of the gray-haired senior citizen, who gave the appearance that after a life of more chips than fish, bending down and standing might be her main forms of daily exercise.

"Hello," Sloane began. "I was wondering if one of you two could help me."

Even though she stood squarely in front of the woman, the man ambled over to her while the woman turned her back to Sloane. "What can I do for you, young lady?" His expression was warm, as his sweater vest rebelled and stretched over his barrel belly to reveal an untucked plaid button down.

"I'm doing some work at one of the houses along the coast for the new owners. They are interested in the history of the house. Can you help me with that?"

He smiled politely, looking at the other librarian to see if she was watching. She gave him a tight-lipped scowl that clearly said, "Say nothing. She's an outsider." The old man sighed as he turned back to Sloane.

"Which house are you talking about? And what do you want?"

Sloane handed him a piece of paper with Brian and Rin's address as she ticked off her mental list. "Anything you know would be great. Records of previous owners, newspaper clippings mentioning anything to do with the former tenants, birth records, death records…"

He held up his hand. "Now just slow down there, miss. You're acting like I know how to use these newfangled devices. I'm a retired fisherman who likes to read. That's all. Now Abigail here, she…" He turned to gesture at the other librarian, who was walking away, her broad backsides swinging as she hurried.

"Doesn't want to help me apparently," Sloane supplied.

"You're probably right. I can show you the microfiche room where you can go through every newspaper this town has ever published. Might take a while though." He winked.

"That would be lovely, sir."

"Call me Bud. Everyone else does."

He led her to a dusty corner room with stacks and stacks of microfiche, some labeled and some in stacks still waiting for their final resting place. There was also an old viewing machine. He clicked it on, and they listened to it hum to life.

"What house was that again?" Bud asked.

Sloane gave him the address.

"You mean the old Whitcomb place." He went out to the shelves and started skimming the titles on the plastic binders.

"What place?" Sloane asked. "I haven't heard anyone call it that before."

"The Whitcomb's were one of the founding families. They were around here forever. Donated the land for the town square and the grade school."

"Oh, and why don't they live there now?" Sloane said a silent prayer of thanksgiving. This man was a wealth of information.

"Died out, I think. Last one I know of married one of my best friends and moved away. Since then, there hasn't been a Whitcomb in Yarmouth."

Sloane's back was to the door, but she knew when someone else entered the room. She turned to find Brian standing behind her.

"Hey, Sloane. Gossip around town is that you're at the library," he said. "Sorry, bad small town joke. I saw your red convertible out front. Sticks out like a sore thumb. Am I paying for that? And if I am, what are you doing here?"

"Research," Sloane responded. "Bud, this is Brian Monroe."

The men exchanged a firm handshake.

"The local paper fiche is over here." Bud pointed. "You know how to use one of these?"

"Of course. Is there any chance you might give me your own knowledge of the place? Or maybe a month or year when something about the place might have been in the paper?"

"I've lived in this town a long time. Talk is gossip,

and that's not something I'm prone to engage in."

"How about facts? Can you share any facts with me?"

Bud pulled a binder from the shelf and handed it to her. "Some of my best friends lived in that house, and I miss them a lot. You might want to start there. I think that might have the information you're looking for, Miss…?"

"Osborne. Sloane Osborne."

"It was nice meeting you, Mr. Monroe," Bud said, heading for the door. "Good luck with that house."

Brian settled into the seat beside her as Sloane flipped the machine on.

"I saw Rin last night," Sloane said.

"What do you mean?" Brian's voice was cold.

"She's in the mirror, just like you said. And there's a shadowy thing there with her. I don't know how she got in there, but we have to get her out."

"You saw my wife, and you're doing here doing research?" Sloane could hear the anger and frustration in his voice. "You said you were getting a hotel room."

"Look, every second counts if you want your wife back. So stop second guessing me. I need to know what I'm dealing with," Sloane explained. "I can't help her until I know what I'm up against. Are you going to help me or not?" She gestured to the machine next to her.

Brian slumped in the chair with a sigh, flipping the machine on.

Hours later, a famished Sloane had nothing. Nothing significant anyway. Nothing in the way of murders, hauntings, or rumors. The binder Bud had given her was full of information. She'd barely touched the fiches filed inside, and she'd been scanning the pages forever.

And Brian was no help. All he wanted to do was complain.

"Are you really going to sit here all day?" Brian whined, pacing the room. "Shouldn't you be looking for Rin instead of staring at old newspaper clippings?"

Sloane turned to look at him, trying not to be mad. His bald head shone brightly under the fluorescent light, and his chin was still sprinkled with the same stubble he had last night. Hadn't he bathed or slept either since she last saw him? She supposed she wouldn't be finding any peace either if someone she loved was missing.

Turning back to the viewing monitor, Sloane almost clicked past the article on the page, but stopped, leaning closer to the screen.

'That's them," she said.

"What?" Brian stopped pacing to come look at the screen. "Who? Do I know them?"

The old black and white picture had faded before being scanned onto the fiche, but there they were. The man and the boy from her dream. She could see the smile lines on the old man's face as he beamed at his son who held a fish almost as big as he was. The article was titled *Local Fishermen Win Prize for Best Fish at Fair.*

Sloane studied the boy. He was the same as she remembered from the dream. If that was the case, then they must have died... Sloane raced through the documents. She knew what she was looking for now. And there it was. Just days later in August of 1927.

There was an article with the title "Waiting in Vain." The top half of the words were faded as if someone had spilled water onto the page, but Sloane read what she could.

Common scene after fog and storms...went out when weather...turn for the worse. After the...hurricane passed one fishing boat has yet to return. Even in our modern world, tragedies befall us...as is with much of the history of our proud town, we know...remains to see if the bodies of twenty-two-year-old Joseph and his father, forty-three-year-old Samuel will be found.

Her cell phone beeped in her bag, and she picked it up. The message was from Whitney.

—Emergency. Come outside NOW—

"We need to go," Sloane told Brian gathering the microfiche and placing it safely back in its binder before shutting down the monitor.

"What's going on?" Brian asked.

"Not sure. Whitney said it's an emergency."

"Who's Whitney?"

"Local girl. She's helping me out."

Sloane thanked the librarians who didn't even acknowledge her exit. Fresh roasted coffee beans assaulted her, and the immediate desire for a cup of coffee became a need, not a want. Too bad she didn't have time. Whitney was waiting right out front.

"Hey, Whitney, this Brian," Sloane greeted her. "He owns the house."

"Nice to meet you," Brian replied, though his sour look didn't agree with his words. "What's the rush?"

"The Besses and Hank are headed out to the house right now," Whitney explained "They are trying to mess things up for you!" Whitney was visibly trembling. "I can't believe them! Hank told Kevin last night, but he didn't tell me until now, and I didn't want—"

"Whoa, hold up. What are they planning to do?" Sloane asked. This was low. She knew the group was unprofessional, but to mess with someone's work was beyond the limit. She had a lot of expensive equipment in the house. She didn't even want to think about what she'd do if something was ruined.

"I'm not sure, but I wouldn't put anything past them."

"Do these women drive a black SUV and hang out with a tall man who looks like he's had the life sucked out of him?" Brian asked.

"Yes," Whitney replied. "Why?"

"Because I'm assuming that's them." He pointed up the street to where a black SUV turned the corner, but not before they caught a glimpse of the *Yarmouth Ghost Hunters* sign on the side of the vehicle.

"Come on, Brian. We're going after them. Whitney, you call the police before following us. I want them observed in the act of trespassing so the police will give them a citation."

Whitney pulled out her phone.

Sloane and Brian made good time heading back to the house in her rental. There was no way they'd have time to do too much damage before she caught them.

Pulling up to the house, Sloane had a bad feeling. Like sinking, drowning, and hopelessness all at the same time. She could see the house from the end of the drive, but something was off. One of the Besses, the one Sloane thought of as Tiny, was up on the widow's walk, and Hank and Skeletora were nowhere to be seen. That probably meant they were inside, rifling through Sloane's stuff.

"What the hell, man! They shouldn't be in my house. It's dangerous in there. Those idiots are breaking and entering!" Brian jumped out of the car as soon as it stopped, sprinting toward the front door.

"What are you doing? Wait for the police!" Sloane called, but it was too late. He was already inside.

Whitney's old Impala slid into the drive followed by the squad car. Sloane met them as they parked, glad to see there were two officers on the scene.

"Hello Officer. I'm Sloane Osborne." She shook one of the officer's hands.

"Nice to meet you, ma'am. We were called about a breaking and entering," the officer replied, reaching up to rub one side of his thick black mustache. "Are you the owner?"

"I'm working for the owner. He's the man who just ran into the house. We believe there are at least three others in there who shouldn't be. Two women and a man. One of the women is up on the widow's walk." Sloane pointed toward the roof.

"Get away from me!" Tiny yelled, pulling Sloane's attention back to the house.

Sloane squinted to see better Tiny wasn't alone up there. A shadow of some kind came in and out of focus. A human shaped shadow with glowing eyes.

"I'll go in and check it out. You stay here and question her," the officer directed his partner. He started for the house, and when Sloane went to follow him, the other officer stopped her.

"I'm going to need to ask you a few questions," he said.

A gut-wrenching scream came from the widow's walk. They both looked up.

"What is that?" the officer asked, "Please let me go in. We can talk after everyone is safe." Sloane turned to head for the house but was stopped cold.

"Help! Hank!" Tiny sobbed, her voice cracking.

Her small body was flung back and forth like a rag doll by an unseen force as if she were purposely flinging herself across the widow's walk... With a crack, the old metal railing gave way, and she fell backward with a gut-wrenching scream.

Time slowed. Sloane was the first in motion. Running toward the house. But there was nothing she could do. She watched in helpless horror as Tiny slid down the roof, her hands scrambling on the worn shingles. She reached the edge where the leaf-chocked gutter connected with the house, and for a moment, Sloane thought she's be able to hold on until someone could get up there to help her.

The gutter cracked and Bess screamed for help as it detached from the house. Her body connected with a thud to the lower roof of the front porch, and Sloane heard the sickening snap of bones before Tiny Bess rolled off the roof and smacked into the ground.

Sloane continued sprinting the rest of the way up the path.

"Get an EMT here," Sloane yelled over her shoulder. The officer barked requests into the walkie-talkie attached to his breast pocket. A few seconds later, Sloane heard the wail of a siren in the distance.

Chapter Seven

Whitney was on Sloane's heels when she reached Tiny. The woman's small body looked even more petite when bent at odd angles. Sloane didn't know much about medicine, but she could tell this was bad. Blood pooled around Bess' open wounds and slowly seeped into the grass. Both of her legs stuck out at odd angles, and Sloane could see the white of a femur poking out above her left knee. One arm was bent under her, the other thrown out to her side. Sloane could see her eyes rapidly moving behind her closed lids as if she was trying to look everywhere at once. A low moan wheezed from her mouth, more like an exhale than a word.

"She's alive," Whitney breathed, leaning close to Bess' face. "Bess, honey, can you hear me? It's going to be okay. It's Whitney. I'm right here, and the paramedics are coming. You just hold on."

"Bess, can you hear me?" Sloane asked, leaning as close to the small woman as she could without actually touching her. "I know something was up on that roof with you. Did you see what it was?"

Tiny's body shuddered, and she moaned in pain.

"Leave it," Whitney admonished, turning on Sloane. "Can't you see this isn't the time for your work? She's hurt and…"

"EEEE…VVVV…IIII…LLLLL." Tiny's voice

was so low Sloane wasn't sure she'd heard her right. The woman's eyes shot open, her pupils dilated until almost all the color was gone, and leaving black holes starting straight at Sloane.

"What did you say?" Whitney asked.

"EVIL," Bess said more clearly, before her eyes rolled back in her head as she fainted.

With a loud cry, Skeletora ran out of the house, Hank on her heels, shoving Sloane and Whitney out of the way. As they crouched beside Tiny, Sloane couldn't help but notice Skeletora Bess' lipstick was slightly smeared on Hank's face.

"What happened?" Hank asked.

"She fell off the widow's walk," Whitney answered. "Where were you two?" Her tone was accusatory.

Hank ignored her, reaching out to cup his wife's cheek in his hands.

"Don't touch her," Sloane snapped, and he jerked his hand back. "You might make things worse if she has a neck or back injury."

Bess made a gurgling noise. It sounded like the cross between a whimper and a gag. Sloane glanced down the hill. An officer with an EMT badge on his arm was already on his way up followed by a couple of paramedics with a stretcher and a neck brace.

"What was she doing up there anyway?" Skeletora asked.

"I don't know," Sloane said. "You tell me. You were the ones with the great plan to break into the house. I was hoping you'd know what she was doing. None of you should have been in the house, let alone on the roof. What'd she do; catch you two going at it and run for it?"

Sloane grimaced at Skeletora's guilty expression. Maybe her wild guess wasn't far from the mark. But this wasn't the time, and she couldn't wait to give her testimony on how Whitney had known they were going to be in the house.

A wet pine cone flopped to the ground beside her, and Sloane looked toward the roof. It was a long way up. A flash of color caught her eye, and she leaned back so she could see onto the widow's walk. A glimmer of a shadow, and then it vanished.

The paramedic knelt beside Tiny, as they covered her with braces and splints before easing her onto the stretcher. Sloane eased back, knowing she was no use to anyone. Behind her, she heard the two officers talking.

"Where's the owner?" an officer asked. "The one who claims his wife is '*missing*'?"

"Didn't he run into the house?" the other man supplied. "I saw him go in as we were pulling into the drive, right before Sergeant Todd. Then the woman fell."

"I see what you're saying, but would he have had enough time to get all the way up there?"

Oh, no! They were right. Brian wasn't making his case any easier the way he was acting.

Sloane looked up to the widow's walk, and sure enough, Brian was leaning over the broken banister. Exactly the place a man in his situation should not be. Behind him, Sloane could make out the murky edges of a shadow. A deep pang of fear dug into her chest, and she was running before she thought about the consequences. She dashed up the porch steps and through the front door, just as the officer was exiting. If he tried to stop her, Sloane didn't hear. She had to get to Brian.

Sprinting through the house, Sloane took the stairs two at a time, cursing when she had to slow at the winding staircase leading to the widow's walk. The door at the top was closed, the lock drawn from the inside, something Brian could not have done. Sloane felt panic tightening her chest. Her breath came in short wheezes as she tried to control her fear.

As Sloane pushed open the stout wooden door, she heard a rasping chuckle, almost a harsh wheezing noise. She stepped onto the walk, and a shadowy figure that was blacker than black turned to look at her. Brian was oblivious, standing near the rail—too close considering the wind and the fact that someone had just fallen.

The entity wrapped itself around Brian before turning toward Sloane, red eyes blazing with the darkness it held inside. Deep endless pools of torture. It was as if the fires of Hell were trapped in the depths of its soul, and Sloane couldn't look away.

Brian turned, jumping when he saw Sloane. "What the hell?" Brian asked. "You nearly scared the life out of me."

Sloane couldn't answer. The shadow receded from Brian and slowly sank through the floor, disappearing into the house below. Sloane watched until it was gone, then she shook herself as if coming out of a trance.

"What did you say?" she asked.

"That poor girl," Brian said. "I heard voices as soon as I got up here, but the door was closed. I tried to get through but something…laughed. I think it pushed her. Holy hell." He ran his hands over his bald head.

"We never should have bought this house. First Rin, now this. It's cursed. Look at this." He gestured to the broken railing.

"What about it?" Sloane asked, moving closer for a better view. "It's broken."

"Yes, but look *how* it's broken," Brian said. "Usually when metal snaps, it's a clean break. This looks like it was… I don't know, melted or something."

He was right. The metal looked concave, like someone had taken a blow torch to it.

"It looks like it was tampered with," Sloane admitted. "The police are going to need a statement. What were you thinking, running into the house?"

"I was thinking, 'this is my house! Get out of my house!'" Brian yelled, turning away from Sloane and pounding his fist on the railing, speaking to whatever was haunting his house. "Sloane"—the look on his face verged on crazy—"you have to make it leave. Before anyone else—" He couldn't finish the sentence. He didn't have to.

"Come on." Sloane grabbed his hand, pulling him away from the edge. "We need to get you down before the cops come up to get you. It'll look better if you voluntarily answer their questions."

The cops were waiting for them at the bottom of the stairs to start their questions. It took hours to interview everyone who witnessed Tiny Bess fall. Not wanting to leave the premises while the police were there, Sloane texted Whitney a list of supplies she needed while she waited her turn.

Trying to block the memories of her last interaction with the police, where the chief ended up being a serial killer bent on adding her to his tally of victims, Sloane answered the questions as best she could.

Yes, the door was locked. No, she hadn't been home. Yes, she had paperwork allowing her to inhabit the house during her investigation. No, she hadn't given Bess permission to enter the house. Could she please get a bottle of water?

Brian didn't get off as easily. It was obvious the cops thought he had something to do with the accident, but without sufficient evidence, they couldn't take him into custody, only ask him not to leave town. Again. Now he had Rin missing with a story that the cops would chalk up to him being a nutcase, and another woman "thrown" off the roof of his house. This was getting out of control.

With Rin still out of reach, Tiny in the hospital, and Sloane no further in her investigation than when she started, she squashed the feeling that it all seemed worthless. What had made Tiny go on the roof? Sloane doubted she went up there without reason, even she wasn't that dumb. Not only was it dangerous, but when breaking into a house, you didn't go somewhere you'd be seen.

Sending Whitney and Brian out for supplies, she grabbed her requisite bottle of water and wandered down to the beach once again. Removing her shoes, she rolled up her pants and waded up to her ankles. The water lapped over the cool sand and with each pull outward, it eroded the sand and her feet sank into the surf. The water was cold enough to make her gasp, but Sloane didn't mind. It woke her up, sharpened her senses.

Although she was brought here initially to gather evidence, her game plan had changed as far as the house was concerned. People weren't *considering* buying it, they'd bought it. From what Jonah told her, Brian's wife loved this place and wanted to grow old here. With a spirit tossing people off the widow's walk, no one was safe.

Instead of digging deeper into whom or what was haunting this place, a decision cemented itself in Sloane's mind: she wouldn't waste her time trying to make peace with this ghost—especially not one who threw people off roofs and kicked her out every time she walked inside only to beg her to come back in once she got too far away. The place was mind-fucking her, and it had to stop once and for all. Or no one would ever be able to live in this beautiful house.

The only way to cleanse this house was to center herself and kick it the hell out. Then she'd use all the experience and knowledge she had to find Rin. Time had run out waiting for Jonah's aunt to show up. She had to deal with this thing. Now.

And there was no time like the present. But she needed a sounding board. Was she doing the right thing? She punched in Jonah's digits.

"What's up buttercup?" he answered.

"No sign of your aunt. And I need to cleanse this house. Pronto. There's been an accident. This entity is stronger than I could have imagined."

"Shit, that bad?"

She snorted. "Well, if you call a black mass of energy throwing someone off a roof bad…then I'd go with a firm yes. And having Brian here isn't making anything better. The man flies off the handle at the slightest thing. I'm glad I'm not his lawyer."

"You're joking, right?" He laughed, a short

chuckle that rumbled from deep in his chest, and Sloane closed her eyes. She could picture him with ease, sitting at his desk, feet propped on top of the pile of files he should be reading, his suit rumpled from a long day at work.

She maintained radio silence to let him know she was serious.

"Wait, are you okay? Do you think Brian has something attached to him? Something that made him hurt Rin? Something that might have him turn on you?"

Sloane dug her toes into the sand. The frayed bottoms of her jeans were getting damp. The concern in his voice sent a wave of heat through her body even as the chill wind from the ocean blew in hungry streams.

When had this happened? When had she stopped thinking of him as a friend? When had he come to mean so much?

"I'm fine. You'd know if I wasn't. Another nosy set of ghost hunters broke in the house, and one got pushed off the widow's walk. I saw the whole thing, Jonah. What pushed her was not a friendly and it was broad daylight. And the thing is, I feel like the house is messing with me. I feel a pull to be inside when I'm not, but once I'm in it's like my mind finds every excuse for me to leave. I feel like I'm losing my mind. It's nuts."

Sloane heard his chair creek as he sat forward and his feet hit the floor.

"Is the girl who fell going to be all right?" he asked.

"Not sure. It was a three-story fall. So I'm done investigating. I need to clear this house to make it safe for Brian and Rin. Tonight."

89

"Gotcha. Well you know how to smudge and salt, but you need to talk to my aunt to make sure you do everything right. She can be there as soon as tomorrow. Are you sure you don't want to wait for her?"

"No, I got this. I'll call her if I need to, but serious question, okay? I know all about your aunt and what she does, but is she really a witch?" Sloane knew all the stories about his aunt, the reclusive eccentric that the police department often called in on cold cases. Rumor had it she was psychic, sensitive, and perhaps even the leader of a Wiccan coven. All of which were just fine. Sloane only wanted to know what she was getting herself into.

"You say 'witch' like it's a bad thing. There's probably a witch or two among your ancestors, so don't harp on my aunt. And for all my 'gifts' you might as well call me 'Jonah the warlock.' Although, like a Christmas Catholic, I am not technically a practicing warlock."

She giggled. "Very funny. But can't I just smudge, light candles, use the holy water and salt thing, and tell the bastard spirit to leave?"

"Sure, but it might not work. Want to get it really pissed? Do a half-assed cleansing." Jonah paused. "Listen, wait a few days, and I'll find a way to get away. To come help you."

She refused to be rescued again. "No, I got this. I know I can do it. I only called to run through the basics, but if you think I can't handle it—"

"I never said that sunshine," he interrupted, "I just wouldn't want anything to happen, er... I mean, attack you."

"Please stop acting like you care." Sloane let the

words slip out in a harsher tone than intended.

The blustering wind and crashing waves were almost more silence than she could bear. Jonah wasn't talking anymore.

Shit.

"I do care about you, Sloane." His voice was husky and low. "I care about you more than you know."

Her feet were now buried ankle deep in the surf and her pants were drenched. Firmly stuck in constant movement.

His breathing on the other line soothed her into a catatonic-like peace. "I'll have any information I can dig up on that house in your inbox by tomorrow morning, sooner if I can."

"You can do that?" she asked. "I thought you were too busy with your super important case."

"I am busy," he admitted. "But you're more important."

Sloane's heart did a little flip in her chest, and she felt a smile curve her lips.

"If you're sure," she said.

"Think about who you're talking to. Of course I can do that. My security clearance can get me almost anything."

"So, if I hear you right, you're telling me you have a new FBI intern who's driving you nuts, and you'll love waking the kid up to make him do the work."

"You know me so well."

She laughed. "Well, call that intern, then go home, have a drink, and go to bed. I bet you slept in your office last night, and you've been up working since dawn."

"Don't you know it? Thank goodness for comfy

couches." She heard him run a hand over his jaw, the rough hairs on his chin bristling against his palm as he sighed. "I am dead tired."

"Good night, Jonah," she said. "Sweet dreams."

"They will be." Was she imagining the husky tone in his voice? "Check your email tomorrow. I'll have that information for you."

"You're the best." Did he know the real meaning of those words when she spoke them? She almost couldn't admit it to herself. And so went another conversation with the one man in her life that felt like a thousand-piece puzzle that never quite fit together.

I hate puzzles.

She disconnected the line and sighed, staring at where the sun's reflection over the water flickering over the waves. It was beautiful, but her mind wasn't on that. She needed a drink way more than Jonah did.

Sadly, it might help her focus on the case instead of the man she... *No, I won't use that word.*

Heading back up to the house, she found Brian and Whitney each having a glass of wine. She poured herself a glass of wine from the bottle they had already uncorked. "Did you pick up those things I asked for?"

Whitney nudged a paper bag on the table toward her. "I already had most of the stuff. I'm a newbie to acknowledging what I'm seeing is real and actually seeking it out, but this is not my first ride on the merry-go-round. I can help you with this."

"Good, I do need your help," she began. As soon as her words were out, a wisp of darkness glided past the kitchen door. Only this time, it wasn't just Sloane who saw it.

"Sloane, there it is again!" Whitney pointed.

Chapter Eight

Setting her wine glass down, Sloane channeled anger and buried her fear. This "being" had *hurt* someone today. Hurt them bad. And enough was enough.

"What?" Brian said. His attention had been elsewhere.

"Did you see that?" Sloane got up and dumped her wine down the sink, rinsing away the crimson color with tap water.

"Hey, that's expensive wine. What are you doing?" Brian said.

"I saw someone or something zip past the door." Whitney rubbed her hands up and down her arms as if to prove her point. "I have goosebumps all over my arms and on my neck."

Before Sloane could organize one coherent thought, her cell rang again making them all jump. "Hello?"

"Is this Sloane Osborne?"

"Speaking."

"Hi sweetie, this is Jonah's Aunt Stephanie. My lovely nephew sure must think a lot of you. He's been leaving me a message every hour on the hour. Called in an emergency favor. But I love that damn kid. So, let's go. Where are you right now?"

"I'm at a private residence in Yarmouth, Maine

where a black entity pushed a paranormal investigator off a widow's walk today. She could have died. I need this thing gone."

"Okay, my dear. Three deep cleansing breaths."

There was a pause, and Sloane waited for her to continue, but the line was silent.

"I said three deep cleansing breaths," Aunt Stephanie said impatiently. "I'm old, not deaf. I know you didn't take them."

Hurriedly, Sloane obeyed, gasping air into her lungs three times.

"All right. Feel better?" the lady asked though she didn't wait for an answer. "Now, to work. Jonah said you want to do a cleansing? Is that because you can feel the malevolent energy inside this house?"

Understatement. "Yes."

"Have you cleared a house before?"

"A few. But in my line of work, most of the time I try to keep the benevolent ghosts around."

"You won't be alone starting right now. I'll send my positive energy your way. And I'll be right there with you, sweetie. If Jonah asks me for something, that's one person I'd cross the ocean for in a hurricane. Ready?"

"I am. And by the way, thanks. I think you have a pretty great nephew, too."

The snort from the other line wasn't exactly a cackle, but it held hints of I-know-stuff-you-don't. "Do you have the stones from Jonah?"

Digging in her pockets, she pulled out the stones. "I have them."

"Go somewhere you can be alone, at peace and separate out the black stones. Those are tourmaline.

They'll protect you. The spirit won't be able to attack or attach itself to you." She coughed, the rough, ragged sound of a longtime smoker.

Sloane put her hand over the receiver. "Can you guys give me a minute?" she asked Brian and Whitney, who headed into the living room. Dumping out the stones onto the kitchen island, she picked out the three black ones.

"Okay, I have them."

"Now, hold those stones in your free hand and close your eyes and imagine the light inside of your soul can extend outward. Pull it out from your deepest consciousness like a string on a yo-yo. Think of the yo-yo as something held firmly inside of you. Immovable. The piece of you that is all you. But imagine you can extend it, and try to visualize wrapping that string of light around you."

Sloane never thought of herself as anyone special. Was she? Or was she just a girl who sold haunted houses? A ghost hunter with fading memories of her parents and fiancé who had an uncertain future ahead of her. Who was she to be able to summon some beautiful light from within that would magically protect her? A terrifying thought struck her. She had no light. She didn't only have nothing outside, no future, no lover. She had nothing within. No light, no spark, no magic.

"Do you see it?" Stephanie said.

"Uh…well." If a magical light ever surrounded her, she'd only felt it once, and it was Michael's light. He owned that light and allowed her to borrow it.

"Tut tut, Sweetie. Listen to me. Jonah tells me your aura is tangerine. And he of all people would know."

I have a tangerine aura? This is something a friend

shouldn't keep from you. She hadn't even known he could see auras, but he should have mentioned it. No time in her life had Jonah ever said anything like, "You have a beautiful glow to you, Sloane. Like a circular orange fruit." This would be good information to have handy for emergencies.

Like now.

Stop distracting yourself! She needed to help Brian and Rin. If she could clear this house, Jonah would be impressed, maybe even proud. She would drive to D.C. and have coffee with him, instead of him constantly hanging out with his partner.

Sloane focused and Jonah's face snapped into view. He extended his hand to her. It was like he was dipped in silver moonlight. She intertwined her fingers in his noticing that her hand did indeed give off an orangish-glow.

She let it seep through her. Bathe and surround her. "I see it now," she whispered, adjusting the phone on her ear.

Stephanie took a deep breath and exhaled into the phone. "Repeat after me: 'I'm surrounded with a shield of protection. I am safe within this space.'"

Sloane did as she was told.

"Time to invoke the elements, my sister."

****

Sloane felt ready to kick some serious ass after she hung up with Stephanie. Imagining herself pulsing with her protective aura, she felt ready to take on the devil himself.

"Okay, you know what?" she announced after she pranced back into the living room, surprised not to find Brian and Whitney, "That's enough. You want to hurt someone? Hurt me!" Sloane Tarzan-beat her chest. Egging on a spirit was never the wisest bet, but in this instance, she could not care less. "I have *nice* people who want to live here. Brian and Rin are good people, and it's time for you to go." She headed back to the kitchen. "Please leave. I'm asking you nicely."

Hadn't she dumped out her wine glass? She even remembered rinsing it with tap water. Yet, there it stood, refilled and calling her name for a sip.

"Want me drunk? Is that it?" She regretted even having a sip of wine before. Alcohol was *not* conducive to cleansing a house of evil. As she reached for the wine, it tipped over on its own, spilling the burgundy liquid all over the island. "Really?" She nabbed a towel from a drawer and wiped up the mess. "This is how you're going to be, huh? Fine by me. I'm about to make your existence here extremely uncomfortable. I may not know what or who you are, but at this point, I really don't care. It's time for you to go."

Even though she wouldn't have minded him being there, Brian couldn't stay. He was too intricately involved emotionally. Where were those two anyway?

Sloane heard voices on the front porch and found Brian and Whitney laughing playfully like old friends. She didn't like it. Not one bit. The damn house at work again.

"I'm ready. Whitney, you can stay. Brian, I think you should leave us. Having you here might piss the spirit off more than help. There's a reason it took her and not you."

"I don't want to leave. Not after everything that's happened." Brian didn't budge.

"I agree with Sloane. It might be for the best."

Whitney's voice rang with sincerity.

After some debate, Brian agreed to leave, saying, "Call me if you need anything. And I mean *anything*."

Glad he didn't put up more of a fuss after she filled him in on her plan, Sloane opened the black duffle bag from Whitney onto the kitchen counter. Time to get to work. She dug out a block of cedar, deeply inhaling the woody scent. She set it down, carefully adding a quarter charcoal tablet and a few dropperfuls of myrrh, frankincense, and dragonblood incense oil. Lighting the carbon tablet, she turned to Whitney. "You ready?"

"You bet." She winked. "Let's do this. Just let me run outside for a minute first and—"

Sloane took her by the arm. "I feel the urge to run outside, too." She pulled Whitney to a sitting position on the floor, and they sat cross-legged facing each other. "We are going to spend a few minutes meditating. Find you inner strength and channel it."

Whitney giggled.

"Shh," she admonished. "Close your eyes and be still. Fight the urge to run. Remember what I said about this place toying with us. Fight the house. Resist your urge to bolt. C'mon, we can do this. Together."

Whitney took a deep breath and nodded. "Okay."

After several minutes in silence and once Sloane felt Whitney was centered and grounded enough to begin, she tapped her on the knee.

Whitney opened one eye. "Ready?"

Sloane lit the incense. "I am going to politely ask you to leave once more, but first, how about a newsflash. You. Are. DEAD!" Jonah taught her to start out at full tilt. The incense mixture crackled, filling the room with its musky scent and heavy smoke. "Ready or not…here we come."

As soon as her shoes met the living room rug, two pictures on the walls began to rattle.

"Think this is bad, do you?" She and Whitney used their hands to direct the smoke to the corners of the ceiling in the living room then headed for the stairs.

Pausing about half-way up, she gave the bowl a little puff of air to get the smoke snaking up again.

The upstairs was quiet. Too quiet.

"You can run, but you can't hide," Whitney added. "We are *not* afraid of you."

Sloane gave her an approving nod. No need to give the ghost insight into her true fears, like the fact that she was terrified of being without water or being left to die in a big hole in the ground.

They worked their way through each room until Sloane stood in the same place where she'd been transported to another time. Whitney worked a few feet away.

The vision had showed her a time when this home teemed with negative energy.

Staring in the mirror, the hairs on the back of her neck and her arms stood at full attention. *It* was here. With her.

"You need to leave." Damn, her voice was shakier than she would have liked. For this to work, the entity couldn't know her newfound confidence was not bullet-proof.

Staring at her own reflection in the mirror, the shower curtain rippled making Sloane jumped.

Then shower turned on…by itself.

Sloane could pretend all she wanted, but she was lying through her teeth. She was scared shitless. And whatever was inside the bathroom with her probably knew it.

"Dammit." She knew she was the only human in this room. But like a bad horror, movie, she felt compelled to check behind the curtain. "Whitney! Get in here."

Setting down the smudging mixture, she turned to the shower. Steam was starting to rise, and the bathroom mirror fogged up.

"Why did you turn the shower on?"

"I didn't," Sloane said, inching closer to the curtain. With a shaking hand, she counted down in her head before she'd whip back the curtain.

Three…

Two…

One! She grabbed the curtain and slid it hard to the right.

Nothing.

Besides an empty shower with the water going full bore at the hottest temperature.

"Fuck!" Her heart thumping, she turned to collect her sage.

With a shaking hand, Whitney pointed at the mirror. Invisible fingers drew on the bathroom mirror, squeaking with each letter.

"G-O."

A cold frost dampened her spirit like an inescapable arctic storm.

"You first," she growled through her chattering teeth.

"Sloane…" Whitney's question hung in the air. Sloane had no answer, no explanation.

After finishing smudging the upstairs, they set the

sage down in the living room and returned to the kitchen. Stuffing their pockets full of tea light candles, Sloane told Whitney to help her light a candle in each room of the house.

Heavy energy settled on Sloane like a yoke on her shoulders. Now she was getting somewhere. Back in the kitchen, Sloane pulled out the holy water and a new container of salt from the bag that Whitney brought. "Sorry about this, but you've given me no choice."

In two tall glasses, she mixed her special concoction of holy water and sea salt.

She found Whitney in the upstairs corner of the house where they began the final part of the cleansing ritual. Dipping her fingertips in the salt water, she let the solution fly off her fingers as she made the sign of the cross and repeated, "I banish all evil spirits from this home in the name of the Universal Creator."

Whitney followed suit until they had repeated the statement in every doorway. She repeated it at every window inside the house, and Whitney went so far to climb into the attic and even by each of the basement windows.

They met up in the kitchen ten minutes later.

"Can you hear that?" Whitney whispered.

She did hear something. It was quiet at first, like a purring cat. She hit record on her digital recorder and carried it in front of her. A black mist hovered in the corner of the kitchen.

"How long have you heard it?" Sloane made small movements toward the corner of the kitchen. The purr turned into a low growl and black mist expanded and throbbed. Whitney clutched her forearm.

Sloane took a step backward and the noise

subsided. It was the same place where she'd felt the presence before. Only now it felt more concentrated. Her one thought was to banish it. But whatever it was seemed pretty pissed they were here and messing with it.

"Where is Rin? I need you to return her right now. We both know you will not be able to return to this realm, and you need to bring her back. In returning her, you regain part of yourself. Perhaps the part you need to move on."

They waited, holding tight to each other. Sloane more out of protection as she sure as shit wasn't going to let another person get taken. If she banished the spirit, they might never find Rin. She needed answers.

If the being was willing to give any.

"I won't ask you again. Where is Rin?"

The black mist expanded and pounced, charging them and passing right through their bodies.

Whitney screamed and Sloane involuntarily shut her eyes.

They spun to find it hovering again in the opposite corner.

"Sloane...look." Whitney held up her arm and three long lines ran down her forearm, where blood starting to show.

"All right, that's it. If you aren't going to cooperate, you don't get to stay!" Sloane lunged for the salt water concoction and flung it at the entity. "I banish you from this home." The being barely reacted, and Sloane wondered if she'd only made matters worse. Then the mist rose into a cloud of black smoke. Fingers snaked out and grabbed Sloane's wrist, immobilizing her as she stared into the black abyss, losing herself. A lot of good the dang protective stones were doing now!

All she felt was endless despair and pain. Sloane sank to her knees trying not to succumb to the cold fear pouring into her soul.

How many cold, dead moments of hopelessness passed she didn't know. She screamed, but it was more like a war cry, encouraging her to marshal all her life force to escape

As soon as Whitney wrenched her free from the entity's hold, it whizzed past them and straight out the front door which had been standing open. Sloane grabbed the salt off the counter and raced after the thing. She opened the spout and drew a thick line in the threshold of the front door.

"The only ones who may pass this threshold are those who are welcome here and whoever they invite in!" She slammed the front door shut and sank to the ground.

Then Sloane let the emotion take her and she wept. She cried for Michael. She cried for what was lost. But mostly, she cried for herself. Whitney sat next to her with her arm around her. Outside, they heard the wind toss trees back and forth, and the distant ocean crashed as if in agreement with her actions. Once she settled herself down, they repeated the incantation at every door and window in the house again before sinking into a deep couch in the living room.

"It's gone, isn't it?" Whitney asked.

Sloane nodded.

Peace.

They could both feel it.

The house was once again at peace.

Chapter Nine

Sloane eased her rental into an open parking space, locked it, and headed inside the diner where Brian was sipping coffee in the furthest booth in the back. "Hey, Brian." Sloane slid onto the pleather seat across from him, rubbing her tired eyes. The cleanse had taken all night, and all she wanted to do was find a bed to fall into, but Brian had called, asking to see her. Of course, she'd driven right over.

The waitress topped off his coffee and placed a steaming plate of steak and eggs in front of him. "You want anything, Doll?"

"Just coffee," she answered, flipping over the waiting coffee mug so the woman could pour. "We did it," she leaned forward to whisper her news after the waitress left.

Brian lowered his voice. "Are you sure?" Plates and cups made tinkling sounds in the background. A normal day for normal people. A life Sloane sometimes envied. But not today. Today she had a piece of good news for once.

"I had to cleanse your house. The entity was malevolent. It was a danger to every person in the house. We had to force it out."

"So it's gone?" Brian's voice broke. "But what about Rin? How will we ever find my wife if you kicked out the ghost?"

The whole restaurant turned to stare at them, and Sloane felt her cheeks heat up. "We're still working on that but at least you can go home."

"Happy? Happy to live in a haunted house that swallowed my wife?" He pushed his food away.

"I'm still going to find her, Brian," Sloane coaxed. "But the house wasn't safe for investigation at this point. Someone was going to die. You saw what happened to that woman. I did what I had to do."

"I don't believe that. What if you made things worse? What if we never get her back?" He stood up and punched numbers into his cell. "I'm calling Jonah and you're not getting paid a cent until you FIND MY WIFE!" He shouted, before leaving the restaurant.

The waitress came over to clear his plate. "How about some breakfast to go with that coffee now, Doll?" she asked as kindly as she could. "No worries, I've heard it said that Monroe guy killed his wife and is trying to get away with it. I was almost worried you'd be his next victim. Rumor is that's his third wife, you know?" She said loud enough for the other patrons to hear. "I never heard what happened to the other two. Left him, some said. But now we are all not so sure."

Sloane had to connect her brain to her jaw to close her open mouth. Damn small town gossip. She knew Brian and there had never been a previous wife. No matter what though, Brian was screwed if Rin didn't show up in one piece.

Soon.

"I'm going to toss this and write it off as unpaid," the waitress said. "Are you sure you aren't hungry? Go ahead and eat it."

No use in looking a gift horse in the mouth.

After wolfing down Brian's abandoned meal and leaving a generous tip, she got back in her rental and headed back to the house to get to work. She needed to clean up the mess she'd made during the cleansing and figure out her next step. She might be a little mad at Brian right now, but that didn't mean she'd return it to him in worse shape than when she arrived. Or leave without finding Rin.

A quick text to Whitney about Tiny Bess's status got a reply of "No change."

She pulled over to text back. "Brian doesn't care about last night. Only wants Rin back. I'm going to spend the day cleaning. That's the final step to clear out the negative energy. Then I'll have to decide what to do next. We have to get Rin back as soon as possible."

After dropping thirty dollars at the local hardware store for cleaning supplies, Sloane found herself whistling on the winding road back out to the house.

Flora sat rocking on the front porch, knitting. She gave Sloane a smile and a wave while she lugged her cleaning supplies up the steps to the front door.

"Good morning, Flora. How are you?"

"Morning? Its afternoon now, dear, but I'm fine. I came over to make you breakfast and find out what happened to that poor girl from yesterday." She kept knitting and rocking, knitting and rocking.

"You heard?" Flopping down in the chair next to her, Sloane gave Flora the update on Bess and last night's cleansing. "It's gone. The evil spirit is gone. I think it'll be safe for Brian and Rin now."

Flora, ever the skeptic, gave her tight, unbelieving smile.

"It's more than that. Maybe you won't believe me,

but that thing that happened on the widow's walk yesterday was no accident. And the whole town thinks Brian has killed Rin. Which is a lie."

"Honey, I'm sure Rin is safe, and she'll be home soon. Towns feed off rumor mills. You can debate all day on whether or not ghosts are real but the whole thing just makes me tired." Flora tucked away her knitting. "Anything left you need help with?"

"I've decided to clean this place from top to bottom. Do you have time to help?"

Flora throat issued a hearty laugh. "Cleaning, now you are speaking my language."

Sloane unlocked the front door. "After you," she allowed Flora to go ahead of her.

"I'll take care of the bedrooms on the second floor," Flora said, leading the way into the foyer. "But that's probably all I'll be able to do. Why don't you start on the third floor and work your way down? I'll get my work done and get out of your hair as fast as I can."

****

Cleaning was not Sloane's idea of a good time. Still she knew she'd made the mess so she needed to clean it up. Starting in the attic, she methodically swept the salt, opening the windows to disperse any lingering scents from the different herbs she'd used in the cleansing.

It took longer than she'd thought it would, mostly because she got distracted by the variety of antiques stored in the attic. Antiquing was a closet hobby of hers. She usually liked to look and not buy, so finding a treasure of heirlooms hidden in the top of the house was pure joy. There were chests of old clothes, dating from before the American Civil War through the sixties.

She found an old lantern with yellowed glass that looked like it could have been a signal on a ship. There were also bits of furniture and faded sepia toned pictures of the people who'd lived in the house long ago. Most were water damaged or blurred beyond repair, so she couldn't tell who the pictures were of. Just that they were from around the 1910s or 20s by the style of clothing. The women were mostly in long skirts and the men dusty suit pants and jackets. They were probably worthless but Sloane tossed them in a box anyway. Perhaps there was someone who would value them.

Because she hadn't started until after noon, by the time she finished with the attic, it was already late afternoon. She made her way downstairs surprised to find the bedrooms were already spotless. Flora could work magic when she wanted to. She had made the bed and swept the floors. In fact, the only room not cleaned was the bathroom where the ghost liked to hang out, and Sloane wasn't ready to tackle that one yet.

Ignoring the pang of unease, she headed to the main floor and got to work in the kitchen. She was wiping a layer of salty dust off the kitchen table when she felt the presence return. Her blood chilled as goose bumps pebbled her skin. Cool air stirred the air, lifting strands of her hair and swirling them about her head. It felt like something was right behind her.

A cold breath tickled the back of her neck, making the hair on her arms come to attention.

Impossible! She'd done the cleansing perfectly. Gripping the bottle of wine like a bat, she swung but connected with thin air. She froze, glancing around the room. From the corner of her eye, she caught sight of a dark shape moving past the doorway. By the time she turned, nothing was there.

She followed the shadow only to find Whitney dancing in the living room. Sloane stopped, leaning against the door frame, to watch. She'd imagined it. It was only Whitney's shadow. "When did you get here?"

Whitney didn't respond. At first Sloane thought the girl was ignoring her until she noticed the tiny white buds in her ears, connecting to the music player in her back pocket. Her riot of red hair was loose, drifting about her face as she grooved to a beat Sloane couldn't hear. She held a broom in one hand, using it like a faux-guitar as she spun across the living room, narrowly avoiding the antique furniture.

With a spinning leap, Whitney landed on her knees before sliding across the polished wood floor. The song must have ended because she opened her eyes, a lopsided grin on her face. She saw Sloane and her smile faded as she pulled the buds from her ears and scrambled to her feet.

"How long have you been standing there?" she asked.

"Not long." Sloane laughed. "But long enough. What are you listening to?"

"Bon Jovi," Whitney answered with a grin.

"Really?" Sloane hadn't taken her for a classic rock kind of girl.

"Yeah, really. I'm finished here." Whitney glanced at the room behind her. "You need help in the kitchen?"

"No, that's done too. Only one room left," Sloane answered. "But did you see something in here?"

"What do you mean?" Whitney asked.

"A few minutes ago I swear I felt something again." Sloane drummed the fingers of one hand on her cheek as she thought. "Tell me that's impossible."

"That's impossible," Whitney insisted. "We did the cleansing exactly how we were supposed to, didn't we? There's no way whatever that thing was could be back."

"That's what I thought too." Even as she said it, Sloane wondered if she was wrong. It still felt like there were eyes on her back. Maybe the no-sleep thing was catching up and making her bonkers.

"By the way, I think that lady was here again," Whitney said, pulling Sloane from her thoughts. "An older neighbor lady just came through a minute ago. Said she was going outside. I didn't stop her because you'd mentioned her coming and going before. She doesn't live here, does she?"

"No, but she might as well." Sloane shrugged.

"She introduced herself, before heading out." Whitney said. "She looked familiar. You know how small towns are—you either know everyone or have seen them around.

Sloane was kind of happy she didn't know about small towns. Everyone knowing everyone and getting in your business. Yuck. Anonymity was king as far as she was concerned.

"I love being a Yarmouthian," Whitney said.

"Yarmouthian?" Sloane couldn't keep a smile from spreading across her face. Whitney was definitely different, but she was amusing.

"I'm thinking of coining the phrase." Whitney reached for a bucket of sudsy water. "The dreaded bathroom next?"

"I'll get it," Sloane insisted. "You go home.

You've helped enough. While I was in the attic playing with all the antiques, you were actually working."

"I was wondering what you were doing up there. I didn't think I made that big of a mess during the cleansing." Whitney said. "Hey, I know this is totally unprofessional, but is there any chance you'd be able to get me Brian's autograph. Maybe a signed picture or something?"

"A signed picture?" Sloane snorted in disbelief. "He's not even cute."

"I know he's not, but he wrote songs like Two Heartbeats, One Soul and Soulmate." Whitney sighed like a teenager with her first crush as she walked to the door. "I love his words."

"And I love his house," Sloane admitted, looking around.

"I agree. I'm pretty jealous." Whitney glanced around the house as she slid her arms into her worn black jacket. "If it didn't smell kind of musty and trap people inside of mirrors this house would be perfect. It has so many stories to tell."

"That's a beautiful way to put it. But dammit, it's now time for Brian and Rin to write their own chapters. Together. In this house. And I'm not leaving until they can. It's just…" she paused in thought, "I still have this feeling…"

"What feeling?"

"It's nothing. Now, get home. It's…" Sloane glanced at her watch. "Cripes, it's after seven. When did it get so late?"

"I'll see you tomorrow?" Whitney asked.

"Of course you will. Tomorrow we find a way to get to Rin. I'm not leaving until she and Brian are reunited."

"Until tomorrow then."

Whitney hopped down the stairs and jogged to her car. Had Sloane been that naïve and loving once upon a time? She knew she had. She's been the doe-eyed student drinking in everything Jonah had told her about the paranormal world. But that had been before the accident. Before she'd lost everything and made her first contact.

Now she felt like a hardened veteran girding for battle.

Too bad her battle was against the toilet bowls and bathtub rings and the vast amounts of spotting from the holy water she'd flung everywhere.

Picking up a fresh bucket of hot, soapy water, Sloane headed upstairs and headed down the hall. At the top of the stairs, she paused, the hair raising on the back of her neck. This was getting ridiculous. She knew the ghost was gone, but she couldn't shake the feeling of being watched. When she reached the top, she glanced back down the stairs, stopped, then bent down to try to see better through the banister. Had she caught a flicker of something out of the corner of her eye?

She stepped forward, so she was past the stairway, and then slowly easing back, she peered down the staircase. Zilch.

I need sleep something fierce, she told herself.

The master suite still sent a shiver down her spine. The evil she'd banished might have slept in this room once upon a time, and her grief had created the poltergeist. When she was swept back in time, the entity had shown her how it was created. But that had been a scare tactic. The ghost had wanted her to know it was old and powerful, thinking she'd be too afraid to continue to fight.

But why?

She decided to scrub the room down while the shower warmed, then shower here herself before heading to bed early in the guest bedroom. It had been a long night, and even though she'd slept for most of the morning, for once, Sloane was bone-tired when she was supposed to be.

Turning the shower on to a reasonable temperature, Sloane shut the door to capture the heat before attacking the sink, toilet, and floor with the soapy water. Crouched on the floor to get the salt she'd somehow managed to get behind the toilet, she felt an uncomfortable bulge in her pocket. Shifting her position, she pulled out the bag of stones Jonah had given her. Protection stones, according to Aunt Stephanie

Rolling the bag over her palm, Sloane listened to the stones clinking against one another. Could these stones really be that powerful? Sloane looked at herself in the mirror. And even if they were, did she really need protecting? Or did Jonah just like feeling needed?

The shower mist coated the mirror so her reflection was a hazy outline in the glass. She remembered the words the ghost had written on the mirror the night before.

G-O

"Oh how wrong you were," Sloane said as she set the stones on the edge of the sink and reached for the glass cleaner. "I'm still here, and you're the one who's long gone."

As she leaned forward, the water pressure in the

shower lessened. She swore, dropping the cleaning rag into the sink.

She knew better than that. Old house. Old pipes. She shouldn't have left the water running that long if she wanted a shower.

Turning to shut off the spray, she noticed a slight sound, like fingers scratching on wood coming from outside the bathroom. The hairs on the back of her neck sprang to attention and she felt a cold pit of fear settle in her chest.

"Flora? Is that you?" she asked, her voice loud in the small room. Her throat felt dry. She needed some water. "Brian?"

The scratching sounded again, louder this time, as though someone was digging his nails to carve in the wood, and Sloane knew it was coming from just beyond the closed door. She inched closer, telling herself there was nothing to be afraid of. Crouching down, she tried to peer underneath when fingertips poked under the door, curling around the wood.

Sloane fell back on her bottom, watching in horror as the fingers pushed beneath, trying to get into the room.

The hand was covered in dirt and grime, the nails jagged and blackened as though used to dig through layers of dirt. The fingers pushed farther into the room, wrapping around the door and tugging at the base.

"Who's there?" Sloane had to try twice to make the words come out. Her voice was frozen. She steeled herself. Shit, this was no illusion. The house was still haunted! Or was it. Was someone playing a cruel trick? She was beginning to feel like everyone was against her in the small coastal town.

Turning the knob a little at a time, she dropped a shoulder and leaned against the door. She'd bash into whoever or whatever was on the other side! Expecting resistance when she tried to open the door, there was none. She stumbled into the master bedroom.

The room was empty.

The only movement came from the billowy white curtains floating by an open window.

Sloane stalked to the window, glaring around the room. If this was someone's idea of a joke, it wasn't funny.

She slammed the window closed, enjoying the way the glass rattled in the old frame. She almost wished it would break. That would give the fear and rage inside her an outlet, but then she'd have to pay to fix it, and she couldn't afford that.

Hearing the water pressure return, Sloane glanced over her shoulder at the bathroom. The steam had returned, billowing into the air like fog.

She debated not showering. But that thought only lasted a moment. Not showering would be the same as admitting she was afraid.

Walking with purpose, she pulled her shirt over her head taking it off as she entered the small room. Her hands were on the button of her jeans when the mirror caught her attention. The words written in the shower steam had changed. Instead of saying "*GO*" like it had last night, it now read, "*NOT LEAVING.*" But the writer wasn't done.

As Sloane watched, one by one each letter appeared in new words written beneath the old in an invisible hand.

S-H-E

W-I-L-L

R-O-T

"Oh, hell no." Sloane pulled her shirt back on as she went to the mirror and swiped her hand through the words, leaving a clear streak in the steam. Where the steam cleared, she could see a face beneath the streak marks made by her fingers.

Sloane's jaw felt slack as her mouth dropped open, and she pulled her hand away from the mirror as if she'd been burned. She couldn't think. She couldn't move. She couldn't even breathe. All she could do was stare at the woman's face where she rested as if she was asleep.

Her face was pale and almost gray making the dark tones of her long brown hair and the sweep of her eyelashes against her cheek stand out in stark contrast.

"Rin?" Sloane whispered, leaning closer.

Rin's eyes stayed closed, and Sloane began to panic, not sure if Brian's wife was sleeping or dead.

"Hang in there, Rin," Sloane called. "I promise I'll get you out."

Sloane had no idea how, but she knew she had to save her.

Movement caught her eye, and Sloane watched in the mirror above Rin's head as a dark mass solidified into the shape of a human. Horrified, Sloane tried to move but was frozen to the spot. It was like she was watching her own personal horror movie play out in front of her. This thing had more power than she'd given it credit for.

Rin's face faded, and Sloane's own scared features started back at her from the hazy mirror. The only thing that was the same was the dark figure behind her, Hazy fingers reached from behind to wrap around her neck but they were solid when they touched her. Sloane felt true fear. Not the tingles up her spine she was used to from seeing a ghost, but sweat broke out on her forehead, and a scream froze in her throat. This spirit was going to kill her. She knew that was what it wanted. She'd messed with it so now she needed to be eliminated

Although smaller than her, the thing had inhuman strength, lifting her by the throat until her toes no longer touched the tile floor. As soon as her feet left the ground, Sloane could move again, and she fought with everything in her. She'd been in life or death situations before and she did not want to die. Struggling, she dug her nails into the arm holding her aloft, but the thing didn't seem to notice.

"She will rot," the thing growled, angry and tormented.

Looking down into its eyes, Sloane could almost see the pits of fiery Hell burning in their depths. Red rage and crimson hate seeped from the burning pools, threatening to consume all that was good and pure in Sloane's heart.

Darkness swirled around her, and Sloane saw flecks of black intrude on her vision. She couldn't breathe, and she was losing the battle with the entity.

She couldn't pass out. That would be admitting defeat, and she refused to do that even if her neck felt like it was breaking in two, and she couldn't seem to get even a trickle of air into her lungs. Kicking out, she tried to free herself from its grip, but it was like kicking a cloud. The arm holding her was solid, but the rest of the thing was mist.

Sloane felt herself slipping, falling into a haze of black and red. She was losing herself, her will, and her ability to fight. Bright colors sprouted around her vision. For some reason, it reminded her of a sunset. Of that brief, intense moment when the overwhelming heat of the sun gave way to the power and darkness of the night.

Sloane felt herself inching away from the red light of day and closer to the blackness, feeling the sadness of loss take over. A piece of her almost welcomed the relief.

But a flicker of the innate stubbornness that was essentially Sloane, objected.

"That moment is orange." It whispered in her head.

Orange. Sloane thought. A bright tangerine orange. Like her aura.

An image of Jonah's face flashed in her mind, and Sloane felt her chest lighten. She had something to live for. She may not know the depths of her feelings but they were there.

That thought broke the trance she was in. She didn't want to succumb to the emptiness. She hadn't wanted to die a year ago, and she certainly didn't want to die now. She had someone to live for whether he knew it yet or not.

Scrabbling with her fingertips on the edge of the sink, her hand connected with a piece of cloth. She grasped it like a lifeline and realized it was her bag of stones.

Praying this would work, she swung the stones at the phantom's head. The bag struck with a dull thud, and the phantom screamed a high-pitched harpy-wail that made Sloane's nearly limp body shudder.

The shadow dropped her, and she fell to the ground, sucking in huge gulps of air as she watched in terror as the phantom's face began to smoke. She clutched her neck, not sure how it was possible she was still in one piece. It felt like someone had taken a medieval mace to her throat, attempting to sever her head from the rest of her body.

A small fire erupted on the thing's shadowy cheek. It clawed at its face, screaming even as it sank, dissolving as it disappeared into the floor.

Sloane ignored the pain in her throat and clutched the bag of stones in her hand. Sprinting out the door and down the stairs, after the demon shadow. She hadn't gotten rid of it with the cleansing, but the stones hurt it. Maybe she could destroy it with the stones. But when she reached the room below the master suite—the kitchen—it was empty.

Sloane sank to the floor, resting her head against the wall as she tried to catch her breath. This wasn't a nice ghost. She wasn't even sure it was a ghost anymore. Not after it had gotten past her fail safes during the cleansing ritual.

She heard a buzzing noise as her back pocket vibrated. Only once. A text. She pulled it out and checked. It was a message from Brian.

"On the front porch. Can't get in. Key won't work. You in there?"

Dragging herself to her feet, Sloane ran to the front door, flinging it open and falling into Brian's arms.

"The ghost...upstairs...Rin...mirror," she gasped out.

"Wait? What? You saw Rin?" Brian dropped her

into the rocker and took off into the house, taking the rickety stairs two at a time on his way up.

Sloane took a deep breath. She wanted to tell him everything. About how she failed. And how the spirit hadn't left and she was no closer to finding Rin. But Brian ran upstairs and she could hear him pounding on the bathroom mirror. That type of reaction wasn't going to do them any good.

By the time he came down, her breathing had slowed, and she had control of herself again.

"I didn't see anything in the mirror." Was that accusation in his voice?

"What can I say? It was there." Sloane walked past him, making her way to the kitchen, knowing he'd follow. She pulled a cup out of the cabinet and filled it with water from the tap. Brian sat on one of the wine barrel bar stools, watching her with concerned confusion on his face. After draining the glass and filling it once more, Sloane tried speaking again, her voice stronger this time.

"Turns out I messed up last night. I was wrong. The cleansing didn't work. This place is not safe. Rin is still trapped. She looks like she is dying, and I don't know how to fix it. I'm not equipped to deal with this kind of situation. I don't know what Jonah was thinking…" Sloane went to the hall mirror in the hall to look at her neck. Not only did she sound like she had laryngitis, but dark bruises circled her throat.

"Come upstairs with me. Tell me everything exactly how it happened," he demanded, staring into the now squeaky clean bathroom mirror.

Sloane turned off the water still running in the shower. There was no way she was ever going to use this bathroom for anything again. Not after what had happened. She didn't scare easily, but even standing in the room again, she could feel her pulse racing and her senses go on alert. She didn't want to get caught off guard again.

"I saw her in the mirror." Sloane leaned toward the glass like she'd done before, but nothing happened. "I tried to talk to her. To tell her we'd get her out, but I don't know if she could hear me. Then the ghost came, and it wasn't exactly talkative. Seeing as it was trying to kill me."

"Kill you?" Brian's reflection appeared in the mirror beside her, leaning down to examine her throat. "You're telling me the thing did that?"

"Held me up in the air with one hand choking the life out of me." Sloane felt her bottom lip start to tremble, but she took a deep breath, determined not to cry. "It's a good thing Jonah gave me these stones. Without them, I'd be a goner."

"I'm so sorry, Sloane," Brian said. "I never meant... I mean..."

"What do you mean, Brian?"

"No offense, but when I called Jonah and asked him to send in his best, I thought he would come himself. I didn't know he'd call you."

"But Jonah said you requested me." Sloane was beginning to smell a lying, cheating snake.

"I would never have requested you." Brian stomped out of the bathroom, yelling at her as he headed down the stairs. "Even if I'd known you were still hunting ghosts, I would never have requested you. You're an amateur. I thought he'd come himself with a team of professionals."

"I'm going to strangle him myself the next time I see him," Sloane swore under her breath as she trailed behind him to the living room.

"Where are these reinforcements he said he was sending? I'm calling Jonah," Brian said, pulling out his phone. "You're fired. I need my wife back."

"Wait, you are not firing me. I can still help. We should talk to your neighbor first," Sloane said, grasping for any reason to stop him from calling Jonah and telling him she'd failed. She knew she was missing something. She just couldn't put her finger on what. "Let's go over to Flora's house. She might know more than she's letting on. She keeps showing up here and seems to know a lot about the house."

"What are you talking about?" Brian asked.

"Jonah said a neighbor would be here to let me in when I got here, and Flora was. She's been in and out of here the whole time trying to help. Where does she live?"

Brian grabbed Sloane by the shoulders, turning her to face him. "Sloane, it was our neighbor *Laura* who was supposed to meet you, but she slipped on wet cement and broke her hip. That's why I told Jonah to tell you where the extra key was hidden before they took me in for questioning."

What? Sloane left Brian, heading to the front porch. She needed some air. The world seemed to be spinning out of control. She pushed through the front door onto the front porch and plopped down on the steps. She suddenly wanted a drink. A strong one.

"Ok, Sloane, you're right. I'm overreacting. You're not fired. I just want my wife back. We'll figure something out." Brian crouched beside her. "If we put our heads together, you and me, that girl and Jonah, we'll think of something."

"I don't know how you could actually want my help?" Sloane heard the hysteria in her voice. "I've spent the last couple of days interacting with a woman who doesn't belong in your house."

"What do you mean?"

"I mean, I thought Flora was your neighbor. I've spent a lot of time with her, and she's not the person I thought she was."

"Who have you been talking to in my house?" Brian demanded.

One of the rocking chairs on the front porch began to rock back and forth all on its own. Sloane couldn't see her, but she knew it was Flora sitting in the chair. She probably had her knitting in her lap and was humming under her breath as the needles clacked in time with her song.

Brian turned his head, his mouth dropping open as he watched the chair move.

"Turns out there might be more than one ghost haunting your house," Sloane said.

Chapter Ten

"Flora," Sloane leaned up against one of the support columns that held up the front porch. The beam was cool against her light t-shirt. "Are you here?"

The chair stopped rocking, and the old woman materialized, knitting at a feverish pace with a frown on her aged face.

"Holy shit," Brian muttered under his breath.

Flora finished a stitch and looked at them both. The kindly lady was gone, her features darkened and the knitting needles began to look more like wielded weapons than objects that created fuzzy scarves and cozy afghans. "This is *my* house, Sloane. I've never told you otherwise. *I live here*. No one can make me leave. Not you. Not him or his wife. No one." She returned to her knitting and rocking like nothing out of the ordinary had happened.

"Flora, it's not you who needs to leave this house." Sloane's heart thumped in double time with the creak-creak of the rocking chair. Sloane knew Flora was right. She didn't *have* to leave. Flora was timeless, made of pure energy and the simple law of physics was that energy could not be created or destroyed. But in this case, Sloane needed the energy transferred. Preferably to another plane of existence. The whole time, Sloane had never suspected Flora was anyone other the kindly old woman who lived next door. She was more than a full body apparition.

Usually ghosts didn't have the strength to appear in full form. They were wisps of light or darkness at the corner of your vision. They were sparks picked up by a camera or even differences in temperature noted on a thermal camera or regular thermometer.

This was something Sloane had never heard of, let alone seen, before. The ghost appeared as flesh and blood. Maybe Sloane could reason with her. "There's someone or something else in this house far darker and more sinister in their energy. Do you know who I'm talking about?"

Flora nodded while guilt seeped into her face and her expression saddened. Completing a loop, she rolled her work together and placed her unfinished project and needles in a small bag on her lap that said "Home is where the heart is." Flora leaned forward, looking in both directions before she spoke again as if the dark entity might be listening to her every word. She raised an index finger to her lips. "Course I know. I live here too, don't I?"

Sloane and Brian edged closer. All at once, their every interaction flashed in her mind. Flora never picked anything up or moved anything in front of Sloane. She hadn't even wanted to shake her hand when they'd first met. "Talk to me Flora. Tell me how to get rid of it and get Rin back."

Her fingers continued to fumble with her knitting bag and she averted her gaze from them. "You can't."

"Oh, I can. And I damn sure will." With a deep breath, Sloane willed herself to calm down before her voice became shrill. "I will not only get rid of this malevolent spirit, but I will get Rin back as well. And you need to help us. Maybe that's part of why you're still here, Flora."

"Calm down." Flora put up her hands as if she was afraid of what Sloane would do. "Rin is fine. She's taking a nice, long nap. I've already made sure of that."

"Please help us," Brian pleaded. "We have to get Rin away from it."

"It's not an 'it,'" she began. "It's a she. And she is very angry. I keep telling her to be patient, let other people come enjoy the house while we wait, but she won't listen," her voice hitched. "She won't listen, and I'm afraid the next person she's going to hurt might be you," she said, pointing to Sloane.

Great. Flora was the protective entity all along, and now with the attempted cleansing, Sloane had gone and pissed off the real evil. Though she still didn't understand how the ghost had gotten past her wards at the cleansing. She must have done something wrong, but what?

"I'm afraid she won't leave unless I do." Flora's image began to shift to insubstantial mist, flickering in and out of existence. "I've been fighting her a long time. That day on the widow's walk, she won. And I'm so sorry about that girl, Sloane." Flora lifted her hollow eyes to meet Sloane's.

Speaking of the entity and the truth to Sloane was weakening Flora, who up until now was the best full body apparition Sloane had ever seen. Something was exhausting her, as if she couldn't even talk about the other, more dominant spirit without it attacking. Sloane needed her to hold out. There was still one more question she needed answered. "I want to help, Flora. I can see this is draining for you. So tell me…who is she?"

"I can't…" The older woman's eyes went wide with fear as she clutched her bag to her chest. "She's coming."

Flora's whole form flickered, and her blue dress turned black and ripped. Orthopedic shoes turned to scaly, decaying feet with yellow toenails.

Then Flora was back, screaming but no sound coming out of her mouth.

Then the beast clawed through her form again, like it lived inside of Flora.

Sloane backed away. The other entity revealed itself. A black mist surrounded Flora, choking her with darkness and consuming her flesh. It covered her body like a new skin, crawling up from her ankles.

Flora head arched back and she screamed as the entity sent her whole body into convulsions.

"Help me," she mouthed to Sloane.

And in a blink, she was gone.

The rocking chair heaved back and forth on its own, a northern gust of wind blowing leaves and sand in tiny funnels around the sturdy piece of furniture.

"That was…that poor lady…she just…" Brian staggered to the edge of the porch and threw up on his front bushes.

Could one ghost possess another? Sloane had no idea. But she did know one thing, this was now beyond her realm of expertise. She needed help.

****

Aunt Stephanie drove a Buick Regal, a gas-guzzling royal blue car that sputtered when it finally decided to choke on its own fumes and clunk to a halt in the driveway.

Sloane went to help her out of the car, but the woman brushed Sloane away and took a long drag on her cigarette before she dropped it, using the heel of her boot to crush it into the sandy soil.

Layered black hair with purple streaks framed her thin face, stopping below her chin in a harsh bob. Her face had a vague resemblance to Jonah's, if he were a chain smoker and had thick wrinkles amplified by heavy foundation. Her eyes matched his and so did her jaw line, though she managed to look feminine.

"Thanks for coming on such short notice," Sloane said.

Aunt Stephanie squinched up her face, assessing Sloane from her dark bangs and down to her tennis shoes. The woman grimaced, and Sloane suddenly felt like she needed a shower, a haircut, and new clothes. Stephanie obviously didn't approve.

"My bag is in the trunk." Stephanie started up the stairs to the house, leaving Sloane behind. "And I called Jonah. We'll need him here too. You've made a mess of this, but we'll figure out a way out. That's what I'm best at, after all. Cleaning up the messes other people have made."

Sloane tried to respond but couldn't manage to get words past the lump in her throat. She wanted to cry and throw up at the same time. She popped the trunk and lugged the paisley luggage up to the main house. *She called Jonah? Great!* Just once, she'd like to be the one running to *his* rescue instead of the other way around.

Sloane took a deep, calming breath repeating her mantra: *In with the good air, out with the bad air.*

Since the cleansing incident, Sloane had done her

research on the woman to make sure she knew the truth and not just rumors. Turns out most of the rumors were true. She couldn't find any concrete evidence the woman practiced Wicca, but Jonah's Aunt Stephanie was the regular psychic of the Buffalo PD, and even freelanced as far away as New York City. According to Jonah, she lived in a modest home in Lily Dale, New York.

Lily Dale!

Of course, Sloane had heard of it. The place was touted as the largest spiritualist community in the world, Lily Dale was full of mediums and psychics who had to prove they have special skills to live there. There was even a fee for nonresidents to enter the town when they held metaphysical workshops.

Sloane found Stephanie trolling around the living room, cigarette in her hand. She left no stone unturned, picking up things at random, moving pictures, and even glancing under the rug. If Sloane didn't know better, she would think the old lady was a thief scoping the place out.

"What are you doing?" Sloane asked, dropping the luggage just inside the front door.

"Getting myself acquainted. Joni should be here in the morning. I need to connect my energy to this space and center myself tonight so tomorrow, we can stir things up and vanquish that son-of-a-bitch."

Joni? Really? She called him Joni? Like the girl's name? And he let her?

Honestly, Sloane was a tad excited to see him even if she was mad at him for lying to her about Brian requesting her by name. Really mad. But she could almost get over that if he was a tad excited to see her too. That is, if a "tad" was like a "holy-crap-lot."

"When you get a chance, put my bag in any room except the bedroom by that bathroom you had trouble in. I want to investigate that one before we go any farther," Stephanie interrupted Sloane's daydream of a "run-and-jump-into his arms, I-missed-you reunion with Jonah."

"Yes, ma'am." Sloane thought about saluting but couldn't muster up the courage. Instead she dragged the luggage to the base of the stairs before following Stephanie into the kitchen. Even after such a short distance she was sweaty and cross, the beginning of a headache starting just below her right eye. This woman was like a gypsy drill sergeant. It was going to be a long day.

Stephanie was in the kitchen. She filled the teakettle with water from the sink. The gas stove made clicking sounds when she turned the knob before the flame traveled in a small circle to light the burner. The woman opened the correct cupboard on the first try and retrieved two mugs while tut-tutting the vineyard-type décor and small wine refrigerator. "You didn't drink any of this wine, did you?"

Sheepishly, Sloane shook her head. She'd wanted to, after all. And probably would have if she'd had the chance.

"Well don't. Understood?" Jonah's aunt wagged a finger at her.

Sloane was already reevaluating her image of Jonah's aunt. She'd expected this super amazing mystic. Instead she got a dry downer who was about to enforce her own prohibition on the house. Not cool.

Crinkling her nose in disgust, Sloane retreated back

to the luggage. The suitcases weighed more than her, and she did her best not to leave scratch marks on the staircase. She resisted the temptation to drag the woman's belongings up each step, but instead she lifted the vessel of immense weight carefully up one step at a time until she had to mop her brow by the top of the landing. She picked it up with both hands, going as fast as she could down the hall toward the flowery spare bedroom. What on earth did the woman carry in her suitcases?

Good, Sloane thought as she placed the bags on the bed. *Let her have this room. It looked like someone had puked dusty flowers all over the walls.*

Hurrying back to the kitchen, Sloane found Aunt Stephanie with another cigarette. The ashes, she tapped into an empty soup container she must have fished out of the garbage. "I really don't know if Brian and Rin smoke or if they—"

Stephanie held up her hand. "They want their house safe? Well, I need a cigarette. Too damn bad. It helps me think."

"I could look for an ashtray?"

"I'm fine. The water is ready. Can you make the tea?"

Almost simultaneously, the kettle began its shrill whistle. "Why can't I drink the wine?" Sloane added a heaping spoon of sugar to their teacups and stirred.

"One more teaspoon, please."

Sloane sweetened up the hot tea a little more before placing the steaming beverage in front of the older woman. What a load of laughs she must be to have around, knowing what everyone is doing even if their back is turned. Sloane had a childlike desire to whip around and give her bunny ears. But Auntie Miss No-Nonsense might not have liked that.

With the utmost adult-like restraint, Sloane refrained from releasing the giggle bouncing around inside her head.

"You need all your mental faculties intact for what we need to do. And if you are impaired in any way, the evil can get inside of you. It will latch on to whatever weakness you have and feed on it to wear you down."

Sloane blew on her tea before taking a tentative sip. "I will remember not to drink before an investigation." *But afterward, I will drink as much as I fucking want.* "Attachments are unpleasant."

"That they are, sugar. That they are. Now start at the beginning. The very beginning. The call you got from my nephew."

Sloane launched into the story leaving out the part about her know-it-all attitude and refusal of local help causing some of the problems. "I do feel partly responsible for the injury. I should have let the local paranormal team help me here. They know more about this place than I do."

"Hogwash, child. Amateurs confound investigations."

Sloane let out a long breath. It was great to hear reassurance that she'd made the right decision.

"Not that you're any different than them, being an amateur yourself. Seeing ghosts doesn't make you an expert, dearie."

Well then. Aunt Stephanie could sure giveth the compliments and taketh them away. Sloane pushed down the desire to retaliate and regale her with her many years of ghost hunting experience. She squished the air out of her ego like a deflated air mattress and shoved it into a box.

"You only recently became sensitive, is that correct? After *years* of investigations?"

"Well, yes, but—" Sloane started.

"But nothing. I was born sensitive. Your gift will take years to cultivate and refine."

And age, Sloane thought. *Like a fine wine.* A sudden urge to uncork a bottle and wrap her lips around the opening and chug entered her multitasking mind. She could get drunk and forget about haunted houses and spirits possessed by other spirits...

Oh, yeah. That was definitely a theory she wanted to bounce off her. She could almost like the cocky lady if she wasn't so strict and slightly terrifying.

Aunt Stephanie clutched Sloane's hand and gave her a squeeze. "I don't like many people. And you probably can't tell because I'm a crotchety old lady who's stuck in my own ways, but I like you. Sort of. I'm not going to do anything nice like get all huggy or anything—unless you're family, I don't hug. And I wasn't sure until meeting you if this was the right thing to do, but I'm going to help you. For Jonah."

"Um...thanks?" Sloane felt at a loss for words. Did this mean they'd be travelling cross country together in a mystery machine solving cases?

****

"You're an asshole," Sloane said the minute Jonah stepped out of the car the next morning.

"Really? That's how you're going to greet me?"

"I'd rather punch you in the face, but I know I'll regret it when my hand hurts." She scowled at him, crossing her arms over her chest. He looked good. Too good, especially when she was mad at him even if she was glad to see him. Sort of.

"What's this about?" he asked, his eyebrows crinkling in confusion.

"Brian asked for me by name?" Sloane prompted.

"Oh that." Jonah at least had to decency to look embarrassed. "Well, he would have if he'd known how good you are."

"Good try," she sighed. "And try telling that to your aunt. She's…"

"Great! Isn't she?" Jonah crossed his arms to mimic her as if daring her to say a word about his aunt.

She shrugged, knowing it wasn't worth the fight.

"Look, Sloane, in all seriousness, I knew you needed to be here when Brian called," he said. "I don't know why, but you are the one who is going to find Rin and get this house back to normal."

"Oh really?"

"Yeah, really. Now stop being a baby and get over here and give me a hug." Jonah picked her up, giving her a bear hug before placing her on the steps and taking a seat. "Now what were you saying about my aunt?"

He looked different than she was used to seeing him. She was used to the t-shirt and jeans look he sported hanging out with Michael or all black when they were hunting ghosts. He still looked good in his wrinkled suit, his broad shoulders pulling at the fabric as he stretched his arms and squinted in the sunlight. His cheeks were marred by a day's growth of stubble and his deep brown hair blew in the breeze coming in off the shoreline.

"I was going to say she's 'weird,' but sure, let's go

with 'great!'" Sloane laughed. Honestly, the woman could run a séance and channel an alien at this point. Sloane was simply elated that Jonah was here!

They lapsed into silence, and for a moment Sloane felt awkward. Her fiancé, Michael, had been Jonah's best friend. With Michael gone, Jonah was her one connection to him, but somehow she'd stopped thinking of Michael and how much it hurt for him to be gone every time she looked at Jonah. Now she saw the man who'd come to her rescue when she'd needed it most. She saw someone who would walk through fire for her.

Sloane knew she was a loner. She hadn't always been this way, but since she'd lost Michael, she'd sort of shut out the rest of the world. Jonah was the only one she didn't have to try with. He knew her, so she didn't have to remember to be herself, if that made sense. She could just *be,* and he was all right with that.

It was probably the fact that she was way over her head with this investigation, but seeing Jonah seemed to set her world back on track.

The sound of his voice soothed her.

His teasing words gave her joy.

And his hugs consumed her.

And maybe—just maybe—it was time she admitted he was more to her than just a friend.

"God, I missed you," she finally said, breaking the silence. As soon as the words were out, she wished she could take them back.

He surprised her by reaching out and cradling her face with his hand. A tenderness twinkled in his brown eyes. She wasn't imagining it. He cared about her.

Say something! she silently begged. The beachy wind blew his hair in all different opposing directions.

He pulled her into another tight embrace.

The brine of the sea filled her nostrils and the roar of the surf her ears, but her senses decided to overload on one thing only…Jonah.

"Sloane, I…" he started.

"Joni!" The woman's timing was impeccable. Jonah dropped Sloane like a teenage girlfriend after she finally puts out. Stephanie swept down the stairs off the front porch, with a hop in her step and a smile on her weathered face. When she reached him, she pinched his cheeks with both hands, just like the dreaded aunt from all the bad Christmas movies. "Look how big you are! Never met a food you didn't like, eh?"

Jonah swept her up, swinging her meager frame in a quick circle.

"Put me down, you rascal." Stephanie's voice was stern, but she couldn't manage to keep the amusement off her face. "And have I given the two of you enough time to catch up? I've been waiting upstairs since I sensed your approach, but I knew you'd need a moment."

"My auntie, always the thoughtful one," he said, in some odd East Coast brogue Sloane had never heard him use. The word auntie came out more like 'ontie.' "It's so wonderful to see you again. Better yet, *work* with you again." He winked.

Secrets, secrets are no fun. Secrets, secrets hurt someone.

"Oh, when did you two work together before? On a case?" Sloane asked.

"Police business, no big deal," he said.

Stephanie swept a dramatic hand over her forehead as if about to faint. "No big deal? You only helped crack open one of the biggest child trafficking cases in U.S. history!"

Sloane felt excluded. She'd never heard this story.

Maybe they would fill her in tonight over a glass of…water.

Yee-mother-fucking-Ha!

"Joni, as glad as I am to see you, much less to work with you again, it's really Sloane you came rushing here to see. Isn't it?"

"Well…I…" Jonah stammered, glancing between Sloane and his aunt.

Sloane almost felt sorry for him. But she didn't need to dig out a hand mirror for confirmation that her cheeks were flushed, too. The woman spoke the blunt truth. At this point, Sloane was beginning to appreciate how she was not one to mince words.

"Stephanie," she chided. "Jonah is here for Brian. We need to find his wife."

"Think what you want, but I see big things happening between the two of you."

They exchanged looks.

"Big things."

Chapter Eleven

A séance.

Stephanie wanted to do a real, full-blown séance to discover what had happened to Flora.

Sloane had never been to a séance before, but she knew it was where a group of people who fully believed in ghosts gathered to create a welcoming atmosphere for a medium to make contact with spirits. The most Sloane had ever done was play at a Ouija board when she was in high school. She was interested to see how Stephanie, a true professional, would run one.

At Stephanie's command, the master bedroom attached to the bathroom where the presence had appeared to Sloane would be the séance room. Sloane was pretty sure the woman would have opted for the bathroom itself if it could have fit the table and chairs inside.

The room was large enough to push all the furniture to the sides and still have a table in the center of the room. The walls were a pale green with long, sheer white curtains that looked like Halloween ghosts if you glanced at them too quickly. Sloane didn't like the room. There was something clinical about it, and she could sense more than one person had died there. They had moved on, but she could still sense the sickness and age that had pulled them over the brink between this world and what lay beyond.

Between a ritual cleansing which involved a lot of scrubbing, salting, and whispering to the house itself while setting up the room, Sloane had spent most of the day trapped in her least favorite place in the house. Luckily Jonah showed up in time for the manual labor. With his help, she'd pushed the heavy wooden dresser and end tables up against the wall under the window. Jonah helped take the bed apart to store it in another room, giving them plenty of space for the table.

At Stephanie's insistence, the heavy oak table was lugged up from the dining room. According to the expert, the circular shape was perfect for a welcoming atmosphere. If that was the case, Sloane didn't understand why she didn't keep a round folding table with her at all times. That would have made life so much easier. Still, she did as she was told, covering the table in black linen and surrounding it with six straight-backed chairs for each of the participants.

Jonah had been strangely quiet since their reunion hug. The few times Sloane tried to speak with him, they were interrupted by his aunt. Something was wrong.

It had to be bad if it was taking this long to get it out of him. Maybe he was moving? Or he'd decided he couldn't put his career on the line to help her out anymore? There were hundreds of things it could be. Sloane was determined to figure it out, but she knew it would take some coaxing.

They draped the furniture with cloth and Sloane busied herself arranging candles around the room as the midnight hour approached. Stephanie wanted the room bright but did not want "harsh fake light" as she called it. Only candles would do. Luckily the woman traveled with a trunk load of tea lights, so Sloane had no trouble placing them on top of every available surface. She hummed to herself while she worked since Jonah wasn't talking. It made her feel a little less awkward. His silence was making her self-conscious. Not that he noticed.

She needed to break the ice, but how? What would get his attention?

Jonah slouched at the circular table, left leg thrown out and right hand resting on the table, his fingers tapping out a rhythm as he stared at something Sloane couldn't see in his other hand.

"Do you think this is really going to work?" Sloane asked, trying to start out with a simple subject and get him talking.

"Is what going to work?" Jonah didn't even look up.

"The séance, of course." Sloane sighed. Small talk wasn't going to inspire him to talk, she'd need to think of something a little more inventive. "What else would I be talking about? Our non-existent sex life?"

That got his attention.

He looked up, his brown eyes meeting hers but instead of the laughter and the well-aimed barb as she would have expected, twin pools of sadness stared back at her. His mouth was working as though he had something to say, but no words came out. Sloane set down the candle she'd been holding and went to him, kneeling beside the table and reaching for his hand. He pulled it back, clenching it into a fist.

"What is it, Jonah?" she asked. "What's wrong?"

"Nothing," he insisted.

"It's not nothing," she said, tilting her head to the side and glaring at him. "What do you take me for? An idiot? I know you, and I know something is wrong, so stop moping and tell me what the hell is bothering you."

A smile cracked his lips and Sloane felt her heart jump. She'd done that. She hadn't realized how much she'd missed this kind of interaction since she'd pulled away from the world. Yes, she talked to people, but to make a friend a little bit happy when he was having a bad day that made her feel a rush of happiness she hadn't felt since before Michael died.

"You don't beat around the bush, do you?" he said.

"You know I don't, so I'd think you'd know by now you can't get away with a non-answer with me?"

He looked down again, and Sloane realized he was playing with a thick gold ring on the fourth finger of his right hand. It looked like some sort of heirloom, with a red stone on top and etchings on the side. Almost like a class ring, but more Masonic.

"It has to do with you," he admitted. "And work."

"How could I possibly be involved with your work?" Sloane asked. Jonah worked for the FBI. She wasn't sure she wanted to be involved with his work.

"Well, more with what's happening at work. And with Christa."

"Your partner?" Christa. Of course he was talking about his super-hot partner. Sloane liked to call her Boobalicious, but that was just her green jealous monster side talking. There was no denying the woman had it all: looks, smarts, a high paying job, and a rack as big as Kentucky. Literally.

And Sloane hated that the woman got to spend every day with Jonah. She didn't like being jealous. She'd even tried telling herself to grow up and get over it, but it never helped. As usual, at the mention of her name, a sick feeling moved quickly from her stomach to her throat. "What about her?"

"There's this case coming up, and Christa and I need to go undercover," Jonah said. "A really important case."

"All of your cases are important," Sloane agreed to keep him talking. "You save lives. You've been undercover before."

"Yeah, but this one's different. I'm going to be out of contact for a while. Once I leave here, I might not be able to talk to you until this case is done. Not to mention, this one involves…"

"*Wine!*" Whitney sang from the doorway. "I've brought wine and…" She stopped cold and looked back and forth at them in turn. "Uh, oh. I've totally interrupted a very important moment, haven't I? I could come back. We still have fifteen minutes until midnight."

"No, you're fine," Sloane lied, pushing to her feet and away from the only person she really cared about. No way would she get him talking again now. But this conversation was far from over. It would continue…*soon*.

"Aunt Stephanie doesn't approve of drinking and ghost hunting." Jonah sighed, taking the bottle from Whitney. "I'll run down and put this in the fridge until after she goes to bed." He winked at the red-head, sweeping past her out the door.

As he left, Sloane reached into her pocket, fiddling with the small stones he'd given her. Ever since the incident with the entity, she always had them with her. They helped her focus and made her feel closer to

Jonah. Possibly as close as she was going to get. With a sigh, she started to light the candles lining the edges of the room.

"What was that about?" Whitney asked, following Sloane like a kid who wanted in on the action.

"You mean the wine?" Sloane asked. "Stephanie says any substances that decrease your inhibitions during contact with entities is like an invitation for a spirit to jump inside you. Bad idea. I have to agree."

"No, not the wine." Whitney raised an eyebrow. She'd seen right through Sloane's half-hearted diversion. "Though let's not mention I already had a glass or two at home. No, what I want to know is what the two of you were talking about? That's Jonah, right. The one you won't admit you're madly in love with. He's hot."

Sloane felt anger flare deep in her chest. She didn't want someone else thinking Jonah was hot, even if he was.

"What are you talking about? I'm not *madly* in love with him." Sloane tried to think back through her conversations with the girl. Had she mentioned Jonah before?

"I listen and pay attention. You love him," Whitney practically sang, crossing the room and taking a seat. "But whatever. You believe what you want. Tell me what you were talking about."

"I'm not sure yet," Sloane admitted. "Since he got here, I feel like he has something to tell me, but we get interrupted every time he gets close to spilling whatever is really going on."

"And this last time was my fault," Whitney said, playing with the silver locket on a chain around her neck.

"No, it's fine." Sloane lit the last candle, leaving the six pillar candles on the table untouched. Stephanie would light those during the ceremony. "We'll have time to talk later, I hope."

She was beginning to doubt they'd ever have any private time. There was always something more important going on that needed their attention.

"Where's Kevin?" Sloane asked. "I thought you were bringing him tonight. You know, first real date at a séance. How romantic."

"It's not our first date. Just our first séance. He'll be along in a moment. I left him downstairs talking to Brian. I'm sure Jonah will bring them up with him." Whitney leaned back in her chair, letting her long hair flow over the back. She'd dressed for the séance in all midnight blue, but her feet were bare. She'd probably taken off her shoes when she came in. She looked a little like a gypsy. Sloane was really starting to like the girl. Maybe she would make the perfect partner Jonah kept nagging her about getting.

"I hope the boys get up here quick," Sloane said. "It's almost midnight, and Stephanie isn't one to wait."

"We're right here," Jonah said, returning to the room with Kevin and Brian close behind. Brian looked like he'd aged ten years since the last time Sloane saw him. Deep purple bags hung under his eyes, and his usually bald head had a light fuzz on the sides, though the top was still smooth. He reminded her of a dog she'd once found abandoned on the side of the road. He looked lost and alone, but mostly without hope. Kevin was his exact opposite. A gangly man with a headful of hair and a handsome face behind those coke-bottle glasses.

"I found these two raiding the empty fridge," Jonah continued, turning to her with a glare. "Sloane, what have you been eating?"

"Whatever I could find." Sloane felt a slight blush warm her cheeks. "Mostly leftover pizza. I haven't had time, hence the empty fridge."

"Nothing's ever more important than food," Jonah grumbled, taking a seat at the table. His left side facing the open bathroom door with a window at his back.

"So you're the notorious Jonah." Whitney moved over to the seat next to him. "I've heard so much about you."

Jonah's gaze met Sloane's above Whitney's head, a twinkle of laughter in them that had been missing since he'd arrived. "At least my stellar reputation has preceded me."

"Stellar indeed. Sloane only says good things. Except when she has bad things to say, that is. Otherwise it's all good things," Whitney insisted.

The clock struck twelve midnight at that moment, saving Sloane from embarrassment as Stephanie swept into the room. Even though Sloane knew Stephanie was the real-deal when it came to her job, she could tell the woman had a flair for the dramatic.

Watching Stephanie glide across the floor in a full length gray gauzy dress, Sloane swore the woman had lost her feet somewhere between the doorway and her chair. She floated around the table before stopping behind the vacant seat beside her nephew.

Reaching out a thin, boney hand, Stephanie grabbed Kevin's arm, silver bangle bracelets clinking on her wrists.

"You'll be on my right," she said, pushing him into a chair. "We'll sit boy, girl. Jonah will be on my left. Sloane, start your equipment. It's time we began."

Stephanie sat at the circular table, her position directly across from the bathroom where Sloane had seen Rin in the mirror. Kevin fell into the seat beside her. Whitney claimed the seat beside him, patting his hand soothingly.

Brian sat across from Stephanie, glancing over his shoulder as he took his seat as if half expecting the spirit to appear before the séance began. Sloane pressed record on her voice box and video recorder, before sliding into the chair between Jonah and Brian, completing the circle. Stephanie insisted the equipment wasn't necessary, but Sloane wanted documentation, just in case.

Stephanie leaned forward, striking a match on the stiff black tablecloth to light the six pillar candles in the center of the table. Blowing out the match, she set it on the table in front of her, the tip still smoking. The flickering lights heightened Stephanie's age, shadowing her eyes, and dancing around the wrinkles lining her face. For a moment Sloane felt chills run down her spine. She could see how Stephanie would make a good medium. In the candlelight, she looked otherworldly and a step away from death herself. Ghosts probably saw her as a kindred spirit, and Sloane meant that in the kindest way possible.

Stephanie reached behind her, pulling a gauzy veil over her head. Sloane could still see the woman's eyes peering from inside the cloth, but her face was hidden from view.

"Join hands," Stephanie commanded, reaching for

the men on either side of her. "Close your eyes and clear your mind of all negative thoughts. Focus on only one thing—we welcome any benign spirit who hears our call."

Sloane followed directions, gripping Jonah and Brian's hands tightly. Jonah's hand was warm and reassuring, but Brian's was sticky with sweat. She wanted to pull away and wipe her hand on her jeans, but even an "amateur" like her knew the circle, once made, shouldn't be broken.

As this was her first séance, she didn't know what to expect. She hadn't been able to see the spirits for long—just over a year—but in that time she'd had both good and bad experiences. There'd been the caterwauling young mother on the ranch in Wyoming. The spirit had attacked Sloane at first, demanding Sloane return her baby, but had settled down into a peaceful solitude once she'd learned her son had grown up into a lovely man. Sloane neglected to tell the spirit that her son had died at the age of seventy-two, more than fifty years ago.

And then there'd been the creepy twins in the New York high rise. Just looking at the two boys standing hand in hand in the hall was enough to give Sloane the creeps. They hadn't been precisely evil, just prone to pranks, but Sloane wouldn't have wanted to live there herself. The single entrepreneur who'd purchased the place had been happy enough though.

And, of course, all the women she'd saved in Wisconsin. She'd seen a lot of ghosts in a short period of time, but Sloane grudgingly admitted Stephanie was right. She wasn't like Jonah who'd been sensitive as a child. She was an amateur—no matter how much she hated that word.

Whitney giggled across the table, and Sloane grimaced fighting her instinct to open her eyes and admonish her. She should have told the girl alcohol would invite a spirit in the moment she'd found out. She sighed. Another rookie mistake.

"Clear your minds." Stephanie's voice was a soothing monotone, drawing Sloane in to a drowsy stupor just shy of awake. "And relax. I will begin the séance." With the candles flickering in the in the center of the table as she intoned, "Dear Spirit, bless this sacred place. Let the light of the flames radiate love and protection to all four corners of this room. I ask that any negative energies be released from this space. With a bath of white light, I ask that it be cleansed and neutralized. Turn this dwelling into a sanctuary. May it be the foundation for your teachings and the inspiration for my higher perceptions."

"And now the prayer of welcome," she said, bowing her head.

Jonah had explained to Sloane that prayer was an important part of a séance. Not only did a medium need to ask for protection for everyone at the table but to welcome a certain kind of spirit to the room with you. Without the prayer, anyone could join the party.

"Goddess," Stephanie began, "please bless this table and watch over us as we attempt to discover why your servant, Flora Whitcomb, has been unable to leave this world. And now Flora Whitcomb, we ask that you join us. We summon you with the power of love and light. We welcome Flora to our table to hear her story. Goddess, please keep malevolent spirits at bay until we have completed conversing with Flora. You can now open your eyes if you choose to."

A lump of unease began to grown in Sloane's stomach. She'd done much the same thing when she'd cleansed the house. Her mistake had been allowing Flora to breach the front door from her own invitation. Somehow that had opened the door to the other spirit too. But in Sloane's defense, she hadn't known Flora was actually dead at the time. Pushing down her dread, she focused on clearing her mind of all negative thoughts. Stephanie was an expert. She knew what she was doing.

"Flora." Stephanie's voice dropped an octave, hitting the gravely tones only an incessant smoker can achieve. "Flora Whitcomb. We call to you and invite you to this table with welcome understanding. We want to know your story."

"Sloane."

Hearing Flora say her name, Sloane looked around.

There was no warning. One minute the air behind Stephanie was empty, then Flora was standing behind her left shoulder.

Flora looked the same as always. Graying blonde hair drawn back into a tight school-marm bun, wearing a crisp white blouse over a long gray skirt. Looking at her now, Sloane couldn't believe she'd missed the signs. She should have known the woman wasn't only set in her ways, but from a different time period altogether.

"Flora, I sense your presence," Stephanie said. Sloane glanced at her in confusion then realized beneath the veil the medium's eyes were still closed. "Please speak or give me a sign you are here."

Flora's looked at Sloane's over Stephanie's head,

and Sloane could tell the old woman was agitated. Flora wrung her hands, her form flickering in and out of focus as she seemed to beg Sloane for help.

"Speak for me. I can't do it." Sloane heard Flora's voice in her head as if the ghost whispering in her ear.

"She's here," Sloane said.

Stephanie's head snapped up, darting around the room before her stern glare settled on Sloane who realized Flora wasn't visible to her. Only Sloane could see the ghost and Stephanie didn't look happy about it

"Flora, have you chosen Sloane as your interpreter?" Stephanie asked. "Or has she taken it upon herself to answer for you?"

Sloane tried not to grind her teeth. "I will speak for her," Sloane said.

"Flora, if you've chosen Sloane as your voice, please knock twice." Stephanie lowered her head again as if meditating, leaning toward the table. "If not, knock only one time."

"Oh, for heaven's sake…" Whitney began, until Sloane kicked out under the table, silencing her.

Flora rolled her eyes, then reaching past Stephanie, knocked two times on the table. Sloane had never seen her touch anything except her knitting bag.

"All right." Stephanie's sigh told Sloane she was resigned to the situation. "You've made your choice. Now tell us what happened to you. Why haven't you been able to move on?"

Flora's agitation increased as Sloane waited for an answer.

"I couldn't," she finally said and Sloane repeated her words for the rest of the table. "They never came home. They said they'd be home, and I must wait for them."

"Who didn't come home?" Stephanie asked.

"I can't...won't..." Sloane couldn't convey the desperate sadness she heard in Flora's voice.

"This is unnecessary," Sloane told Flora. "It's only making everyone uncomfortable. You can trust these people. Appear to them. Be brave, Flora. You can tell us anything."

There were gasps around the table as Flora appeared to everyone. She stood completely still, her gaze focused on the center of the table.

The candles on the table sputtered, then the flames grew, emitting puffs of smoke which spirals together until it became a wispy ball, hovering over the small round table.

"Aunt Steph, what is happening?" Sloane heard Jonah's whisper from across the table. "I've never..."

"Shhhhh..." Stephanie hissed. "Keep your mind open, Jonah." As the ball of smoke spun, strange lights began sparkling inside of it until, like a crystal ball, images formed. Everyone stared at the ball in the center of the table, as Flora's life enfolded before them.

The woman sat at a kitchen table set for three with platters of food lain out all around her. A storm battered the house, thunder shaking the foundations, and lightning streaking past the windows as the wind screamed at the seams, trying to get in. Flora stared out the window into the tempest, tears falling without stop as she watched the storm rage.

The scene changed and Flora, dressed in black sat between two black draped tables, a handkerchief in her hand, but her face void of tears. On one table was a gold framed black and white photo of a middle-aged man. He was handsome in a rugged outdoorsman sort of way with a thick mustache and beard almost concealing a half smirk and bright, mischievous eyes. Sloane recognized him from her dream. This was the sailor lost in the storm at sea.

The other table held a picture of a young boy on the cusp of manhood in a matching golden frame. He was the other person from the dream, and Sloane knew immediately who he was. It's obvious the boy was a combination of Flora and the bearded man. From his straight jaw to the twinkle in his eyes, he was the perfect mix of the two. Even in the black and white photograph, Sloane could see the restless energy in him. The picture was even slightly blurred at his feet, highlighting his inability to sit still long enough for the photo to be taken.

Sloane sensed Flora's anguish. It was still palpable. Even after all this time…painful to relive.

My Samuel.

And my Joshua. My baby boy.

Sloane heard the words echo through her head but didn't repeat them. She knew Flora wouldn't want her to.

The images in the smoky ball moved faster, taking the séance table through Flora's time as a widow. In life, she'd never stopped mourning, wearing heavy black skirts and high-necked black blouses buttoned to the collar even in the heat of summer.

And every night, she set the table for three.

A steady pattern formed. A penchant for depression and powerful anger as Flora refused to admit the truth.

They were not coming back.

The image faded from the ball of smoke, and the candle flames shrank back to normal size. An uneasy silence hung over the small room until the bathroom door slammed shut with a vicious crack. Sloane jumped, feeling her heartbeat quicken and the small hairs all over her body stand on end.

She knew this feeling. An entity was close. Sloane looked to her left, past Brian to the closed bathroom door. The spirit was close, but at the same time, Sloane felt something else. Suddenly Stephanie stiffened, sitting up straight in her chair, eyes wide beneath the gauzy veil.

"I hear another spirit," Stephanie said. "A second voice is calling. He wants to come in."

"Who is it?" Flora wanted to know.

"It's an older man. Samuel, he says…"

"Samuel? My husband?"

"Well, welcome him already," Whitney said, earning a stern glare from Stephanie.

"Samuel. We welcome you to this table. Please come in peace that we may deliver any messages you have."

A tall man flickered into view as he floated through the outside wall behind Stephanie He was easily recognizable as the man from the picture at the funeral. He reached toward Flora, a sad longing on his face.

"Flora, my love." The man's voice was raspy with pent emotion.

"Nooooo!"

A burst from the bathroom, diving through Samuel and forcing him to disapparate. The darkness moved to Flora, towering over her as she cowered in fear, as she tried to avoid contact with the dark figure.

"You dare?" The shadow growled. "You shouldn't even try."

"But you told me you wanted them to come back. I thought you missed them, too." Flora's image flickered as she quickly lost power, being drained of all she was by the presence in the room.

"I want nothing to do with him. You are all I need to survive." A deep female voice rasped with uncontained mockery.

"What do you mean?" Flora raised a hand to her face to wipe away her tears.

"You alone feed me with your pain and loneliness. You make me stronger. And the girl's not out of my reach. She is not hidden from me, as you believe. You have failed."

"What do you mean? Who did she hide?" Stephanie's voice was still calm, as if this sort of manifestation happened all the time. Sloane wasn't sure how Jonah's aunt managed it. Sweat dripped from her brow and her hands trembled. It was all she could do to keep a grip on Brian's hand. He kept trying to pull it away, and she knew not to break the circle. "I didn't want her to get hurt." Flora wrung her hands, pleading with them. "I put her somewhere I thought she couldn't be touched. But, I guess... I don't know... How did you find her?"

"You can't keep anything from me," the red-eyed shadow sneered. "And now she's mine."

"Who?" Stephanie asked again.

The poltergeist rounded on the table, its red eyes searching each of the people until settling on Brian.

"You know who I'm talking about." The creature pointed at him and then toward the mirror in the bathroom.

"How dare you! Release my wife." Brian stood, trying to pull his hands away from Sloane and Whitney, but they hung on. Sloane was glad Whitney knew not to let go. Breaking their bond would dismiss the protections Stephanie had put on them and allow the entity access to them.

"Sit down." Stephanie's voice was stern. "Do not break this circle. This is a peaceful gathering."

Brian didn't look like he wanted to listen, but Sloane tugged on his arm again until he sat, keeping his hold on Whitney's hand.

"We ask you to leave us in peace. This circle is protected." Stephanie told the ghosts.

Evil laughter filled the room as red eyes turned to the table. The dark spirit floated about the table, coming to rest inches from Stephanie's face, its red eyes glaring into hers "Tut, tut, witch. But don't forget, it was *you* who invited me. I don't have to go anywhere."

"We invited Flora," Stephanie said. "Not you."

"I am Flora. Her agony created me." It laughed again. "And this is my house. I no longer want you here."

Chapter Twelve

"This is more than a poltergeist, isn't it?" Sloane knew all about the spirits. Usually they were ghosts of people who had died with something left unfulfilled. They were angry spirits that caused mischief. But this case was different. She'd heard that poltergeists could form off a living person's negative emotions, but this was the first time she'd seen one.

"Yes and no, Sloane, a poltergeist would have been dismissed when Flora passed on," Jonah explained. "This has to be something different."

"But what? How?" Whitney's voice was quiet. She sounded terrified.

"I remember now," Flora whispered. "When I was dying, you came back inside me."

"I did." The spirit said. "So we could be together forever."

"This is a dwelling for the living," Stephanie insisted. "There is no room for your evil here."

"You're wrong," the shadow said. "This is a house of the dead, and *your* kind is not welcome."

Sloane didn't know what made her turn to her left, a sixth sense maybe, but she watched in horror as the door to the bathroom burst open, and the mirror began to flicker, melting and changing until an opening appeared; a black pit of doom, lined by a burning red. From within the void, Sloane could hear echoing screams of the torments and the shrieking laughter of the ghouls.

"No." Stephanie stood, still holding hands with Jonah and wide-eyed Kevin. "This house is not your portal to the world of darkness. We forbid it. Take your unclean ways and find a home elsewhere."

"But I have something you want."

The evil spirit gestured to the bathroom, and the portal disappeared. In its place was the image of a pale, pregnant woman. She pounded on the glass, tears streaming down her face.

"Rin!" Brian twisted around backward in his seat to see into the bathroom. Sloane managed to keep a hold on his hand, but Whitney was forced to let go or get pulled across the table.

"Oh, do you want her?" The ghost floated above Brian's head. "I can give her to you, if that's what you want, but I'd need something in return."

"Anything," Brian cried. "I'll give you anything you want. Take me in her place, just let her go."

"I don't want you. But a trade will work. I'll take Sloane."

Sloane's jaw dropped open in shock. What did that creature want with her? She could only imagine the pain and suffering a being formed from negative emotions was able to inflict.

Bile rose into her throat, and she sucked in some deep breaths to stay calm and settle her stomach. She didn't want to be traded, but at the same time, she knew she couldn't let Rin stay there when she could save her.

Before she could talk, Jonah stood.

"You may not have Sloane. We will find a way to release that girl without trading her." His tone was harsh and broke no argument, like a man used to getting his way. "You will leave this place now. Sloane is not yours."

"She's not? Well, then, if you insist…"

The portal winked closed as the shadow dove toward Whitney, disappearing into the girl's body. Whitney fell back, her hands going limps at her sides as her eyes rolled back into her head. She began to shake. Not just shivers but full body contortions that moved the whole table, putting out the flames on two of the candles.

"Brian grab Kevin's hand," Stephanie yelled. "We must close off the circle if we're going to help her."

Kevin reached over and grabbed Brian's hand, his face a mask of terror as he stared at Whitney's convulsing body.

The shaking stopped suddenly and Whitney's eyes popped open. Her mouth opened to scream, but no sound came out. As if a rope was attached from her stomach to the ceiling, she began to rise into the air, her body bending and contorting backward until she was almost bent in half. She started to spin, her long red hair and the tips of her toes just missing the remaining candles' flames as she revolved above the table.

"Goddess, please protect this girl and rid her of the evil that has taken hold." Stephanie's voice penetrated Sloane's shock, but she couldn't bring herself to join in. She heard Jonah and Kevin repeat the prayer, but Sloane knew that wouldn't help. This wasn't a normal possession because this wasn't a normal ghost.

"Whitney," Sloane called over the other voices. "Whitney, can you hear me?"

Whitney's body stopped with her face hovering

upside-down inches from Sloane's. She blinked revealing the red cat-like slit in her eyes instead of the normal blue Sloane was used to.

"Whitney isn't here right now." The voice coming from her friend's mouth was not her own. "Can I take a message?"

The mockery pissed Sloane off. This was a real person the spirit was playing with, and Sloane didn't find it funny at all. Releasing her grip on Jonah's hand, she reached into her pocket, pulling out the bag of stones he'd given her for protection. Acting more on instinct than anything else, she put her hand in the bag, feeling around for a stone. One felt warmer to the touch than the others, so she pulled it out and touched the smooth purple stone to Whitney's forehead.

"No message," Sloane said. "But you can get the hell out of my friend."

The reaction was instantaneous. A scream echoed from inside Whitney as her body straightened. Sloane held onto the stone, fighting to keep it connected to her friend's forehead. She could feel the darkness battling to keep its hold, but Sloane concentrated, thinking only of her love and respect for the tormented girl.

The poltergeist leaked from Whitney, like black smoke pouring from her body; it escaped as a black mist from her eyes, nose, mouth, even her ears, before forming again across the room. Whitney fell, Jonah and Kevin managing to catch her before she smashed into the table.

The shadow screamed in rage, diving into the floor and disappearing from view.

Sloane felt herself falling, suddenly too tired for her legs to hold her. Jonah's arms wrapped around her, lowering her safely into her chair. But he didn't let go, one hand resting on her shoulder and the other holding on to hers.

"Are you all right?" he asked.

"Don't worry about me," Sloane said. "Worry about Whitney."

Kevin cradled Whitney in his arms. The girl was unconscious, but breathing normally.

"Has that ever happened to you before, Aunt Steph?" Jonah asked, glancing at his aunt.

Sloane laughed without humor. She'd just pulled a shadowy, evil entity out of her friend with a rock. If that had happened before, she'd eat her hat. And Jonah's too for that matter.

"No," Stephanie admitted. "I've never encountered anything like this before. When Sloane told me there was a woman trapped in the mirror, I assumed she'd been drinking and was seeing what the ghost wanted her to see. I guess we can conclude this is more than a mere haunting."

"Flora would be a mere haunting." Sloane bristled. She may not have been sensitive her entire life, but that didn't mean she was an idiot. She knew what she was doing and knew when she was in over her head. "Flora I could have handled. That other thing is why I called you."

"I see," Stephanie said. "And I also know how to get rid of it."

"You do?" Jonah's head snapped up, his tone surprised.

"Yes, we must merge the beings back into one to dispel the malevolent entity."

"How do we do that?" Sloane asked.

"Both spirits must be forced into one living body. Then the evil can be exorcised leaving the good half, Flora, and the live participant unharmed."

"Live participant? Who?" Sloane was afraid she already knew the answer.

"I believe the poltergeist has already chosen the living body we must use to house the spirit." Stephanie's eyes drifted to Whitney's limp form.

"Damn." Sloane thought that pretty much summed it up.

****

Even Stephanie seemed shaken up after the séance, putting the room back as it was with shaky hands and awkward silence.

Thinking it best, Sloane suggested Kevin take Whitney home to rest as soon as they'd revived her.

The poor girl had no memory of the ordeal that had unfolded or the role thrust upon her if they wanted to clean up this haunted house.

Whitney laid her head on Kevin's shoulder. "My head is killing me. You"—she pointed at Sloane—"better tell me everything tomorrow. Promise?"

"We'll have a long talk tomorrow after you get some sleep, missy," Sloane chided, giving her a quick hug. How do you tell someone that a ghost needs to possess you to put its good and bad sides back together and move on to the next realm?

With any luck, Kevin would break the news to her in a gentle fashion, and Sloane wouldn't have to do it tomorrow. A cop out, for sure, but better than the alternative. Obviously she needed to ease into the mentor role Jonah wanted her to assume.

It took until almost four a.m. for the rest of them to

clean up and get the room back in order. "I'm beat," Aunt Stephanie said. "If Whitney is willing, I can end this. But first, we need rest."

Brian pulled Sloane and Jonah aside. "I'm staying here. I can't leave Rin."

Aunt Stephanie yawned. "My belongings are already in the guest room." Jonah's aunt had the ears of a bat. "Even though I'm so clearly unwanted here by the spirit. Oh well, too bad." She spoke the words loud enough for the both the living and the dead to hear.

Sloane would have thought the old woman was talking about the ghost if she hadn't thrown a cool stare over her shoulder at her nephew.

Sloane took a seat next to Jonah on the front porch steps staring down at her hands and listening to the waves crash against the shoreline. She shuddered from the cool, eastern wind, and Jonah draped his arm over her shoulder, tucking her against his side. The warmth and protection radiating from Jonah's simple gesture made her melt into his shoulder and wrap her own arm around the small of his back. "You tired?" he asked.

"You know I'm tired. Of course, being a professional insomniac allows me to always be tired but still function. Unlike Aunt Stephanie, I'm not so sure I'll drift off to peaceful slumber in that place." She directed a backward thumb toward the house. She stared out at the moonlight shining on the ocean water. The reflection made a silvery path on the sandy beach making it look like a fantastical bridge leading over the water to another world. It was so different from what was inside the house.

And not the nice side. Not the fluffy clouds, dressed in white other side.

The side for tormented souls.

Nope, she'd rather sleep on the beach than go back in that house tonight.

"How about a fire on the beach? Just you and me," Jonah suggested.

It was like he'd read her mind. She didn't think he could do that, but it was always a possibility. "That's the best idea I've heard all day. I'll grab some blankets from..." She had no idea where to find blankets they could use on the beach.

"Try Aunt Steph's car. She always has some in there," Jonah suggested.

"Are you sure?" Sloane wasn't sure the aunt would stand for sand on her stuff.

"I'll wash them myself. Come on, it'll be fun."

"All right. If that's what you want."

While she ran to the car, Jonah gathered firewood from the stacks outside the house and carried a few bundles down to the beach.

Working together with Jonah put a skip in her step. While he was busy, she ran inside and snagged a bottle of wine, an opener, and two glasses from the kitchen. Steph wasn't there to reprimand them, but she still felt like a kid sneaking out of the house with their parents' stash of liquor before they were of age. For some reason she even tiptoed outside and down to the beach. A glass of wine after tonight's ordeal was definitely in order. No matter what Aunt Stephanie said.

It was only a few hours until daylight. She found Jonah in a secluded spot where the tall grasses shielded them from the watching eyes of the house behind them, and a curve in the beach left them closed off from both sides to passers-by.

Not that anyone was out for a jaunt on the beach at this time of night.

They were alone. *Finally*. Her feeling confused her. She'd known Jonah for what seemed like forever. They'd hung out together with Michael, and she'd spent countless hours with him on ghost hunts before he'd moved up the ranks to the FBI. They were friends. Weren't they? Her stomach did a flip-flop when Jonah so much as looked in her direction. What was she doing? Was she really ready for this?

A piece of her still felt like she was cheating on Michael, even if he let her go when she'd seen him in Wisconsin. Then there was another piece of her that said she and Jonah being close actually helped the memories of Michael shine brighter. Without Jonah in her life, it might be easier to let go and start over again.

But in her heart, she knew giving up Jonah wasn't something she was willing to do.

Kicking off her shoes, she sat cross-legged on one of the blankets and laid out the other for Jonah, pressing the base and part of the stem of his poured wine glass into the sand until he was ready for a sip. In minutes, he delivered, producing a crackling fire. Once the logs took to the kindling and their background music became the rhythmic influx of the surf, Jonah settled on his blanket.

"So that was crazy tonight, huh?" Jonah started.

She watched the flames dance and move like an unpracticed choreography. The snapping of the twigs as the fire grew and the salty smell of the ocean and roar of the waves carried her thoughts far away from the horrible night they'd just had. "Honestly, that was one of the scariest nights of my life and right now, I don't want to think about it, much less dissect it. I don't even know how I'm going to tell Whitney what she needs to do. And how can I? How can I ask that of anyone?"

"Things will fall into place. They always do," he answered. "And you know, we're all here to help you, even if you always seem to want to work alone."

"I do ask for help," Sloane began, then tapered off.

Looking down at where the edge of the blanket touched the light-colored sand, Sloane felt like that split represented her. She was like the sand, always shifting away when something or someone came near. He was right. She didn't like asking for help. That meant letting someone in. Letting them see the real Sloane Osborne. And she was bad at that.

Feeling his eyes on her, Sloane turned to find Jonah staring at her. Not in a questioning way. Not in an abject way. But speaking with his eyes, saying something to her he'd never said up until this moment.

The word he was trying to communicate hit her like a brick to the chest. *Longing.* Her chest tightened as soon as she realized what was happening. *Uh oh.* In that one instant, she realized all the thoughts and feelings stirring inside her were not one-sided.

Her heart stalled in her chest. Was it possible he could think of her that way? Sure they'd shared that one kiss in Wisconsin, but he'd also just saved her life. What was the term for that? The Florence Nightingale effect? Or was that when someone is sick? It didn't really matter.

Whatever the reason, he was looking at her now as if she was his world, and she realized that's what she wanted to be. Not some friend who called him when she needed help, but the center of what he was and what he would be.

But if she was going to do this, she'd have to do it right. He deserved that. And if that was the case, they needed a fresh start.

"There's something I need to do," she said. "Something I've been thinking about doing since I first got here." Toying around with the idea since Jonah showed up on the scene, it wasn't until now that the moment was right. And Jonah needed to witness this.

She wiggled and twisted off her engagement ring. "I'm letting Michael go. I *want* to let him go." She brushed the sand off her pants and rolled them up. Wading into the surf up to her ankles, she threw the ring. She heard the dull plop when it hit the water.

"Good bye," she whispered. "Thank you for loving me."

Turning back to the beach, she felt a weight had lifted from her. There were no tearful words of good bye. The time was past for that. The finality and reality of his death was something she had at long last accepted. A dramatic gesture. It was almost funny. That ring could have paid for six month's rent. But that didn't matter.

It was time to move on.

She was going to tell Jonah how she felt about him.

He hadn't moved a muscle during the whole thing. Hadn't risen off his blanket, joined her in the surf, or even said a word. In silence, he simply watched her. His stare intense as the firelight danced on his face and his hair was tossed around by the wind. Instead of sitting back down on her blanket, she padded around behind him and sat next to him.

"We both loved him." Jonah voice held no

cadence, no anger. It was a fact.

"I know. But I'm seeing more clearly now. I know what happened in that bar the night we all met." She gulped. *Here goes nothing.* "You are who I was supposed to be with the whole time. From something he said to me in Wisconsin, I believe even Michael knew it."

Jonah reached an arm around her, pulling her right up against his side. "He deserved every moment of happiness you two had together. But you deserve happiness too, you know. Even if he's gone."

She didn't know what to say. "I remember what you said to me while I was in the hospital. There was a bet in the bar on who would talk to me. You won, but lied and told Michael he won. You put him first. It was like you knew he needed to be first. But right now, I want the past in the past. I don't care about tomorrow. I care about right now. And I care about you." Transferring her weight so she was on both her knees, she knelt next to him, running a finger down his cheek.

There was no moving on in her life without first seeing where Jonah stood with her. But both of them tiptoeing around their feelings wasn't getting them anywhere.

Deep in her soul, Sloane could feel the universe shift. Like the cosmic passage of time was waiting for them to finally realize they were meant to be together.

He closed his eyes and sighed. "I care about you, too. More than you'll ever know."

In a swift movement, he had her on his lap, and his lips were on hers. He was a rock of muscle. His unrestrained need for her surfacing as their tongues tangled and explored their new world. He wound his fingers in her hair and gently pulled her head back to look at her. "You have no idea how much I need you right now, do you? How much I've always needed you. Are you sure you want this?"

Instead of answering, she placed her hands on either side of his face, cupping his cheeks in her palms. She took a moment to take in his beauty, the disheveled dark hair, the hard lines of his face and jaw and his dark eyes. She lowered her face down to his until their lips met again. His kiss was warm and gruff, tender yet demanding.

This was the man she was meant to kiss. Like this. Every day.

Clarity as to her true purpose in life washed over her like a tsunami beating against an impermanent beach. Michael might always have a piece of her heart, but Jonah had the other. Sitting in his lap and making out like frenzied teenagers about to be caught by their parents, she brushed her hip against his pants and moaned, wrapping her legs tightly around his waist, never letting his mouth stray from hers.

She backed off of him and grabbed his hands until he stood up. Sliding off the clothes from her lower body, he undid his belt and stepped out of his jeans.

He sank back to a sitting position. This time when she straddled him, she let him sink deeper and deeper inside her, until their cool bodies were one, heat from the inside keeping them warm.

She wrapped her arms tightly around his neck and sank until he was completely inside her. She shuddered with every inch farther that he slid in until they were united.

Then she wanted to freeze time forever. Her body

begged for movement, but she held her position, allowed the lack of movement to have her memorize exactly how she felt with Jonah filling her up.

Now shaking with the urgency of having him move inside her, she released her grip on his shoulders and looked again into his eyes. The longing was still there, but his lids were hooded in the heat of their union.

"God, I love you, Sloane. I've always loved you. And damn you feel like heaven."

Ever so slowly, she began to move. Back and forth, grinding him deeper and then releasing. The heat coursing from her core to her whole body, passing to him and back to her. Her head rested on his shoulder. She didn't want this to end. They continued to move in unison until she could bear it no longer. She welcomed the fall over the edge, feeling his warmth flow into her and her orgasm pulse against his release.

It seemed like forever, that they stayed together, holding each other, panting and shaking.

"Wow," was about the only word she could muster, before they both collapsed on the blankets.

In a wink, Jonah had grabbed the other blanket and they were covered, him holding her in the afterglow of their moonlight lovemaking. Her brain swam. Michael. Jonah. All the years past and the uncertain future. Images of the three of them hanging out where Jonah and Sloane were teasing each other and Michael always wore a certain look of half amusement, half irritation at their behavior on his face.

She felt Jonah kiss her on the top of the head before she drifted easily off to sleep an hour before dawn.

****

The crashing surf and sting of the sun woke Sloane with a start. Still naked from the waist down, she scampered into her clothes and grabbed the blankets. The embers from their fire still smoldered adding a smoky smell to the fabric.

Where in the world was Jonah? Certainly she hadn't dreamt the whole thing. Her mind reeled. Was he getting her breakfast? Were they officially dating now?

Would she like living in Washington D.C.?

Oh, and he'd definitely need a new partner.

Wait. Put on the brakes there Sloane. This was only one night, and she was already imagining a happily ever after. She needed to stop and think a little bit.

Though that didn't mean she couldn't stop and think while looking for Jonah.

She caught herself skipping back up to the house. No small feat in sand.

The sunrise over the coast today had opened up a whole new world. He'd said he *loved* her! That he'd *always loved her!*

Jonah's car wasn't parked next to hers outside the house. Brian's was.

The mystic and the homeowner sat in the same rocking chairs where Sloane had seen one moving on its own when she arrived. If—no *when*—she and Steph cleared this house for Brian and Rin, everything was going to change. She could feel it in her bones. "Morning. Did you see Jonah?" Failing miserably, she tried her best to suppress the blush she knew was creeping up her cheeks at the mention of his name.

Aunt Steph sipped on a steaming beverage from a Styrofoam cup. Her face was creased with lines of worry and almost...was that pity? "He's gone. Called back to work. But he left you this." A piece of paper folded in half. Not even in an envelope!

Sloane,

Last night was amazing. I had to go. Work. Sorry. It might be a while. I understand if you don't wait for me. My life is not conducive for an "us."

Always have been...

Yours,

Jonah

It felt good to crumble the paper in her hand and even better to toss it to the ground. She squelched the urge to stomp on it—and maybe jump up and down on top of it while screaming some choice profanities—but only barely. Suddenly the squeak of Aunt Stephanie's rocking chair became irritating, and the sun was too bright. The sand in her butt became unbearable and ghost hunting felt like a useless profession. Anger overtook her.

She'd *slept* with him! More like jumped him. Maybe it was too much, too fast. Sloane raised her eyebrows at the both of them. "Work, huh?" Aunt Stephanie would probably make up some elaborate excuse about her darling nephew. Beside the fact, she'd obviously read the note and knew everything already. Ugh, and likely so did Brian.

"You're kidding, right?" The background hum of the thud of the crashing waves now sounded more like someone being beaten with a whip. No answer from the peanut gallery. Was this a sick joke? Was Jonah going to jump out from behind somewhere and say, "Gotcha!"

Sloane did her best to level a sneer at Jonah's closest relative.

Aunt Steph sighed. "I'm so sorry, my dear. He's confused by his feelings for you. Give him some time."

After plopping down on the top step of the porch, Sloane dug out her cell phone. If she called him and asked him to come back for her, surely he would. Right?

"Don't do that," Brian said, sitting down beside her on the stair. He rubbed his hands against the thin cotton of his khaki pants, making a shushing noise that only added to her rising ire.

"Do what?" she asked.

"Curl in on yourself. Give up on him," Brian replied.

"Who said I'm doing that?" Sloane knew she sounded like a petulant child. He was right, but that didn't mean she wanted to admit it. This was none of his damn business. And since when was he such a relationship expert, Mr. My-Wife-Got-Sucked-Into-A-Mirror?

"Of course you're going to deny it, Sloane. You haven't changed a bit since college. You'd shut yourself off when things didn't go your way then, and you're still doing it now."

"I'm not shutting myself off." Sloane frowned. Was that really the kind of person he'd thought she was? Sounded like he had about the same opinion of her as she had of him.

"Not shutting yourself off? You're sitting there pouting, but you're not thinking about how you're all alone and you deserve better than this?"

"Really?" She snorted, glancing over at him.

"*That's* what you think I'm doing?"

"If it's not, then what's going on?" he asked, settling himself more comfortably on the steps, with one arm draped across the top step as he stared out toward the ocean. "Wondering how to get him back here?"

"Actually, I'm thinking about how I don't deserve a lecture from you about love. Now go away so I can find out what's really going on here."

She waited for Brian to leave before pulling her phone out of her pocket and staring at the screen. How did she put what she was feeling into a message? She could call him but knew she didn't have the courage. Finally, she settled for the only thing that summed up everything going through her mind and her heart.

Really?

That was the only word she could manage to text him, but her finger couldn't press the send key. She wanted to cry. But there was no crying in ghost-hunting and the hell if she would break down in front of anyone.

"The time for the two of you is not now," Aunt Steph said in her calmest voice. She'd been so quiet sitting in her rocking chair Sloane had forgotten she was there. "It will be soon, but not now. He felt terrible leaving, but the call came in when he came up here to get you some morning coffee. There was a plane waiting for him, so I guess it was pretty important. He cares about you Sloane, more than anyone else."

Her words lessened the sting of the ocean on her cheeks and immediate emptiness in her heart. But they were still just that, words.

And once again, she was alone. At least she was getting good at being alone. Not depending on anyone.

Doing what she wanted when she wanted.

Oh, who am I kidding? Not having Jonah around already made her feel like to-hell-with-this-investigation. "I wish I could go home and bury myself in old movies and chocolate marshmallow ice cream."

"Can I come?" Steph asked. "Look Sloane, we started something here that Jonah can't finish. Are you going to follow through with me or run away? If you stay, I can give you some tips about how to protect yourself in the future and some knowledge about the goddess." She leaned in closer. "I might even show you my Book of Shadows."

Laying her head in her arms, Sloane wondered when it had come to this. From steamy beachside sex with Jonah last night, to prattling on with Stephanie about the spells of protections. Not to mention she was still tasked with forcing the two vestiges of Flora inside a human host in the hope that her spirit could finally move on.

"I don't know what to say," Sloane said, head still buried.

"Well, think on it, girl. And someone is coming for a visit."

Sloane heard the door to the house close right before the rumble of an engine turning onto the drive. She only lifted her head in case it was Jonah.

But it wasn't. Only Whitney and Kevin bearing caffeinated gifts of liquid energy. "Morning, I brought coffee." Her sing-songy voice implied she had no recollection of spinning on top of the séance table the night before.

Damn. Maybe Kevin hadn't told her what had happened, and now Sloane was going to have to do it.

But how did someone start a conversation like that. *Oh, good morning. How are you feeling? Any lingering effects from your possession? No? Well good, because here's what we have to do...*

Not really Sloane's idea of titillating conversation.

Whitney handed a grateful Sloane a cup of coffee before clearing her throat. "So Kevin filled me in on everything. I'm down with it. How do we start?"

Well, that saved some time.

Chapter Thirteen

Sloane paced the master bedroom where the séance had happened the night before. The room looked like a perfect square to her, but Stephanie said they needed everything to be precise so here she was, less than twenty-four hours later, back at it. It might be the middle of the afternoon, but Steph had insisted daylight was better for this task. At least Sloane had a cup of steaming coffee in her hand to help her focus even if her mind wasn't on her work.

Ten steps to the window. Should she call Jonah? She hadn't done much all day but think about him. Ten steps to the bathroom. Would he even tell her why he'd left? The stupid prick. She couldn't even eat. Just picked at her food and it was all his fault. Ten steps back to the window. And should she even care if the bastard who'd had sex with her and left her on the beach had a reason? Ten steps back to the...

"How do I look?"

Whitney leaned against the doorway, draped in white linen from head to toe. She put one hand on the back of her head, pushing her chest forward in a come-hither gesture.

"Like a sacrificial virgin," Sloane said critically.

Both women burst out laughing.

"Steph's idea?" Sloane asked.

"She insisted. And there's something about stones

and candles. I wasn't really listening." Whitney walked to where Sloane stood by the window, leaning on the sill to look out. "I'm too nervous and wound up to listen. I get to be the vessel to put two spirits back together."

"You're excited about this?" Sloane asked. "Listen, Whitney. I'm not sure what Kevin told you about last night but…"

"Oh, he told me everything. I remember most of the séance." She flounced around the room, taking a seat in one of the chairs Sloane had pushed against the wall. "Just not the part where I was possessed and levitated or something. How cool is that, by the way? Listen, did you get it on video?"

"I'm not sure. I can check." Sloane hedged in disbelief. That wasn't something she wanted to watch again.

Honestly, a piece of her was relieved it was Whitney and not her who had this job. The last thing she wanted to do was be part of some sort of crazy ceremony to shove a broken spirit back together. The thought of being possessed by two halves of a conflicted ghost did not sound like a good idea. She'd almost rather be stuck in a pit again.

Almost. Not quite though.

"I know it's crazy to be excited, but I am." Whitney's face lit up with a smile. "I've always wanted to see more than my sister's ghost and to live a life like yours, searching for them, and helping spirits move on or deal with their passing. This is my first chance to be that person."

Sloane stared at her. The girl was practically glowing.

"This is going to be amazing. I bet no one has ever done this before."

"Yeah." Sloane chuckled, sipping her coffee. "I'll be sure to contact Guinness Book of World Records. Do you think you get Guinness beer for life if you're in there? Are you sure you want that?"

"All right, fine. I'll keep it to myself." Whitney sighed, laying a hand dramatically on her forehead as if the world had suddenly become too much to bear. "Besides I wouldn't want to deal with being famous. All those people wanting autographs. I'm not sure I can handle it."

"You can handle being possessed, but you can't handle an autograph?"

"I'm a complicated woman." Whitney stared down at her fingers. Sloane noticed they were all chewed to a nub. Perhaps the poor thing was more nervous than she let on.

"Everything's going to be okay." Sloane knew she should put an arm around Whitney's shoulders and pull her close to comfort her in some way. But her awkward social skills only allowed a chummy punch to her shoulder.

"Ouch, what was that for?" Whitney grimaced, rubbing her shoulder. "You know, I like you, Sloane, but you are kind of weird, you know."

"I'm well aware," Sloane replied dryly. "But seriously, don't worry. Steph is a professional. She knows what she's doing."

Sloane sent up a silent prayer that Steph did, indeed, know what she was doing.

"I know," Whitney said. "Kevin doesn't want me to do this, but I told him I had to. This is a big opportunity for me. And it's to help you. Besides, he and I are only dating. It's not like he owns me."

"Really?" Sloane drew out the word until it was a full five syllables. "Are you two a couple? Not just partners for a séance? I *never* would have guessed."

"Don't make fun." Whitney nudged her with her shoulder. "We've only been together three months. We knew each other in high school, but lost touch during college. It wasn't until we joined the paranormal society that we reconnected. It took me years to get him to ask me out, though it may have just been him being oblivious to the fact I liked him."

Sloane snorted her disbelief. Not only was this Nowhere, Maine, but Whitney was extremely attractive. Kevin would have been an idiot not to ask her out the first time he met her.

"I know," Whitney said. "I hinted and hinted, but he says he couldn't bring himself to believe I actually liked him. I told him I'd take him out for a steak dinner if he took me for a drive in his new car. When we got to the restaurant, he found out I was a vegetarian, and that's when it finally sank in."

"Yet you still like him?" Sloane teased.

"He's adorable, and he has a huge heart," Whitney said, defensively. "But enough about me. What about you and that sexy federal agent? I thought he was going to singe you with his eyes the way he stared at you before the séance started."

"Jonah's protective," Sloane evaded. "We've known each other for a long time, too. He was my fiancé's best friend."

"He didn't look at you like you were supposed to marry his best friend," Whitney said, tilting her head to the side, and lifting her brows with an expression that was both questioning and unbelieving at the same time. "He looked at you like he wanted to rip off your clothes, throw you on the nearest bed, and have his way with you. Personally, with a guy who looked like that, I'd let him try."

Sloane shrugged, her thoughts far away as she stared out the window. She *had* let him try and then he'd left. Maybe he'd gotten what he wanted.

"So, did you?" Whitney asked.

"Did I what?"

"Seriously?" Whitney rolled her eyes, throwing her hands in the air. "You're as bad as Kevin. Did you hook up with Jonah or not?"

"I…"

Sloane was saved from answering when Steph walked in the room. Her flair for the dramatic must have been used up by her outrageous outfit at the séance and Whitney's virginesque robe. Today Steph still wore all black, but it was chinos and a blouse, covered by a long flower patterned shawl. Gold bangles created music every time she moved her arms, and a turquoise stone dangled around her neck. Her eyes were lined with what looked like coal and her hair down, framing her gaunt face and hanging down in lack-luster waves.

"Are we ready to begin?" she asked, her voice cracking. Great, the witch was nervous. That didn't instill hope in Sloane.

"You seem uneasy." Whitney gave a shaky laugh. "If the supposed expert is unsure, that doesn't bode well for a good outcome, does it?"

"Are you certain you want to do this?" Sloane

asked Whitney, trying to give her one last out. "We can always try to find another way to make this work. There has to be…"

"This is the only way," Steph interrupted. "I spent the whole night and most of this morning trying to find an alternative. There isn't one. They must be combined to dispel the evil."

"I'm ready," Whitney said. "I feel like this was what I was meant to do. I want to be able to help Flora move on."

"Then come to the center of the room." Steph placed a glowing incense burner on the table next to the door and dragged a large handbag into the room with her.

"Wait, where are the boys?" Whitney asked. "We can't start without them."

"Seeing as the spirit is female and this is a female ritual of cleansing and merging, I asked them to wait downstairs," Steph explained helping Whitney lay down on the worn hardwood with her legs and arms spread as though creating a snow angel in the dust on the floor.

"Aw, man. Totally missed my moment." Whitney sighed.

"What do you mean?" Sloane knew better, but she asked anyway.

"I was planning on asking Kevin to watch over me and if anything bad were to happen, to mourn my spirit for all of eternity since he'll never find anyone as amazing as me."

Sloane snorted but managed to keep from laughing out loud. Aunt Stephanie did not look pleased. How could Jonah love the crazy woman so much when she didn't have any sense of humor?

Stephanie sniffed her displeasure, a sour look on her face. "The candles, please."

Sloane got to work. Her job was to surround Whitney with a mixture of black and white candles spread exactly three inches apart to help purify the room and instill a sense of peace in the spirits.

Stephanie began a chant Sloane recognized as a cleansing ritual while she poured a line of sea salt between Whitney's body and the candles.

"What are you doing?" Sloane asked.

"I'm grounding her," Steph explained. "Sea salt—never table salt—for the earth, candle for the fire, incense for air." She pulled a glass bottle out of her bag, unstopped the cork, and trickled a bit of water over Whitney's hands and feet. "And water."

"What about spirit?" Sloane asked.

"I see there are some things you do know." Steph muttered. "I have something for that as well." She withdrew a small black bag out of her handbag and poured out six stones. Each of them was a different size and shape. They were like the ones Jonah had given her, but much larger. Four were a translucent gray-black cut into long, thin crystals. One was a round milky yellow stone and the last an irregularly shaped pink.

"The smoky quartz goes on her hands and feet," Steph said, placing the stones on Whitney. "They will keep her aura clean so she can come out of this without a piece of the spirits becoming lodged within her soul."

"We wouldn't want that to happen," Sloane agreed.

"What? You don't like it when I crawl on the ceiling and go all crazy on you?" Whitney tried to joke, as a trickle of sweat dripped down her forehead, heading for her ear. She was more nervous than she wanted them to know. Sloane patted her arm in what she hoped was a reassuring way.

"The citrine rests on her forehead," Steph continued as if Whitney hadn't spoken. "It's used to clarify personal power and energy. It will help Whitney to retain contact with herself when she is invaded by the spirits. And the rose quartz is…"

Steph paused, her hand hovering above Whitney's heart.

"For love," Sloane supplied for her.

"True Love," Whitney murmured.

"Yes." Steph's eyes went wide as she moved the stone over Whitney's prone body. "It's for love. Unconditional love, which I see Whitney is well acquainted with."

"What do you mean?" Sloane asked.

"I mean we cannot do this ritual. We do not have a willing participant." Steph began collecting her stones.

"What? Why not?" Whitney sat up, disturbing Sloane's ring of candles. "I'm ready to do this. I'm a willing participant."

"You may be willing," Steph agreed. "But what about that baby in your womb? Do you really want to risk her life on such a task?"

"A baby?" Whitney's hand flew to her belly. "Are you sure?"

"A baby," Sloane echoed. A tremor of fear went through her. She knew she should be happy for Whitney, but all she felt was dread. "But what about the séance *last* night? Whitney's possession? Is the baby all right?"

Steph pulled a dark purple stone out of the pocket of her pants. She pressed the stone to Whitney's belly and leaned close to the girl as if listening to what the baby had to say.

"You're not far along yet," Steph said. "A few weeks. And I don't sense any negative reaction to your possession. Actually, this little fighter might account for your fast recovery from what happened. In the child, I sense I strong sense of peace."

There go my chances of her being my partner. "What do we do now?" Sloane asked.

Just then Flora walked into the room. Sloane still had a hard time believing she was dead when she was with the old woman. She didn't act like any spirit Sloane had ever encountered before. But that happened in her business. There was always something new and mysterious to discover. Flora was more real than any of the others entities she'd dealt with. Almost as if she hadn't given up on life and still thought of herself as a living person, unlike others who just refused to move on.

"What's going on?" Flora asked.

"Whitney is pregnant." Sloane sighed.

"Well, that's wonderful," Flora exclaimed, clasping her hands in front of her as she beamed at the younger girl. "Motherhood is a life-changing experience. You'll find you become a better person once you have another life in your charge."

"That's easy for you to say. You won't have to change any diapers or endure sleepless nights." Whitney bemoaned, but Sloane could tell from her bemused expression that she was surprised, but happy.

"Yes, this should be a joyous occasion." Steph's

disappointed tone didn't change. "And it would be if she wasn't supposed to be the main player in this melding ceremony for you and your worse half."

"Yes, I can see how that would be a problem," Flora admitted.

"Maybe you could do it, Sloane," Whitney suggested.

And that was the end of their friendship. Right then and there, pregnant or not, Sloane wanted to punch the girl in the face.

"I actually had that idea last night but was afraid Flora had already made her choice. Whitney would have made a good channel, but you will do." Steph didn't seem to have a care in the world.

"Gee, thanks. I will?" Sloane felt her stomach plummet in defeat.

"You've had contact with both of the spirits on several occasions. And Flora seems to like you." Steph was laying it on thick now. "Plus, this may be our only chance to save Brian's wife."

Sloane's heart stuttered in her chest. She just *had* to bring that up, didn't she? *Me? Being used as a vessel to combine two schizophrenic spirits?* This was not something she wanted to do, but she couldn't think of a good reason to say no.

"Strong emotional ties to the deceased will help with the crossing over," Steph replied. "Think of it as a higher calling, or the reason why you were given the second sight. The ability, to move beyond the veil and see what others cannot and the means to free the spirits from their thrall."

"I'm not sure..." Sloane began.

"This will work perfectly. You may actually have

been the better choice all along. I feel that now." Steph ignored her. "Whitney will work as my assistant, and you will be the vessel. I'd rather have Jonah here, but he decided to leave us, so I will have to keep Whitney safe during the process."

But who's going to keep me safe? Sloane wondered.

"All right," she conceded. "But I'm not wearing that ridiculous white thing Whitney has on."

"Suit yourself." Whitney brushed herself off and stood up. "It's actually more comfortable than it looks."

With a defeated sigh, Sloane took Whitney's place in the center of the circle, feeling like an idiot sacrifice to some unworthy demigod. There was no way she was getting out of this so she'd better make the most of it.

Besides, it was the right thing to do. This was her job. She had an agreement with Brian even if Jonah had lied about him asking for her. She was supposed to make this house livable again. And if this was the only way to do it, she'd best buck up and do her part.

Her toes were a few feet away from the bathroom door so she could see the mirror from where she lay. As she watched, a dark hole appeared, ringed by red flames.

"What are you looking at?" Whitney swiveled around to look in the mirror.

"Don't you see…?" Sloane glanced at Whitney. When she turned back the image was gone. "Never mind. Let's just get this over with."

Steph began the ceremony again, ensuring the salt surrounded Sloane's body and dousing her hands and feet in water. Whitney relit the candles, repositioning them to fit around Sloane's frame as Stephanie placed the stones in the correct places on her body, grounding and centering her.

"Now close your eyes," Steph told her as she placed the rose quarts over Sloane's heart. "Focus on your breathing. All you have to do is…be. I'll take care of the rest."

Sloane doubted that but obediently did as she was asked.

At once her senses heightened. The musky sweet aroma from the incense tickled her nose, threatening to make her sneeze. She could feel the cool quartz stones resting in her palms and her feet. The citrine on her forehead was warm against her skin, as if it had been sitting in the sunlight all day. For a moment she thought she could even hear the candles crackling like a real fire burning around her head.

She focused on herself, taking deep breaths in through her nose then slowly exhaling through her mouth, trying to find a semblance of calm. It was like yoga class but without all the hard work. Just the Shavasna at the end—where the world stands still for a few moments. Sloane held onto that stillness. Instinctively she knew if she wanted to survive this, she needed to be calm and in control. And if she was being forced to do this, she was damn well going to do what she could to come out safe and whole.

She heard rustling beside her head and peeked to see what was happening. Steph had settled herself on one side of Sloane's head, and Whitney kneeled at the other, fiddling with the long skirts, trying to keep them out of the flames. Steph extended her arms over Sloane, and Whitney did the same, grasping hands over Sloane's head.

"Flora Whitcomb, you have come to us to be made whole. Tell me, where is your other half. We must have the two to be made one." Steph threw back her head.

Flora reached out, resting her hand over Steph and Whitney's. Squeezing her eyes shut again, Sloane felt a warmth in her chest, like a hug from an old friend. She felt protected. As if these three were a safety net, holding her close. "I am here," Flora's voice sounded strange, like an echoing inside her head. "But I am alone."

Sloane didn't know what Steph thought would happen. It's not like the shadow entity worked on everyone else's time schedule. She wouldn't be at all surprised if Flora's other half didn't show at all.

Wouldn't that be a relief? Then Sloane wouldn't have to be the ritual sacrifice after all.

"Flora," Steph's voice sounded farther away. Muffled and reverberating—as if Sloane's head was submerged underwater. "We're waiting for all of you to join us. You know this has to be done. Do not fight us."

Sloane cringed. That sounded like a challenge and she knew Flora's evil half would relish defeating them. Trying to keep her calm, she concentrated on clearing her mind of everything except Flora's two halves. She pictured Flora's alter ego, driven by hate who lashed out to attack whenever threatened. How different they were. Like two sides of the same coin, only one side was mint perfection and the other scarred beyond recognition.

What kind of anguish would Flora have been feeling to manage to split herself and create a poltergeist from her negative emotions? Not only had she made a new entity, she'd fed that being with her black energy until it was able to remain, even after her death.

Sloane knew pain. She knew what it was like to lose someone she loved. Her parents had died too soon, leaving her alone. Then she'd lost Michael. She knew what it was like to have her heart ripped—still beating—from her chest and to wonder if the pain would ever go away. To want to curl up and die herself, but knowing that wasn't an option. She was more like Flora than she liked to admit, but something had always kept her from following that same road.

Or someone really.

Jonah.

His face flitted through her mind.

All at once she felt a chill up her spine and sensed a thickening in the air above her.

"Thinking of him again, are you?" The demonic voice echoed in Sloane's mind. Her eyes shot open, and she scanned the air around her, careful not to move her head and set herself on fire.

There was nothing there.

But then she heard laughter.

Her gaze met Steph's and the older woman nodded. She knew the other ghost was there.

"I was waiting for a moment like this." The evil half of Flora whispered in Sloane's ear. *"A moment when you'd leave yourself unprotected and open to me. Such things I could do inside your mind."*

"Concentrate." Steph's voice was a cold monotone, her emotions in check. "It wants you to react. It's threatened by you and what we plan to do, but doesn't have any power here unless you give it."

"Yes, calm yourself." The evil entity cackled. A

chilling sound that spoke of horror and humiliation. *"Make your body ready for me, and you'll see what I can really do."*

Without warning, Sloane felt the ghost tunnel into her chest. Her whole body clenched, reacting to the intrusion. Muscles spasmed in her legs, making them board straight and her hands curled into claws. She felt as if she was stretched as tight as she could be, her skin clinging to her bones.

It was too much.

Too much pain.

Too much hatred.

Too much sorrow.

Sloane couldn't handle the feelings pounding through her, swallowing her until she became pain. She felt her body begin to shake as convulsion after convulsion ripped through her, bending her spine and whipping her head back and forth.

"Find your calm Sloane," Steph's voice penetrated the pain though she sounded far away. "You must accept this and let go."

"I can't!" Sloane tried to speak but wasn't sure if any sound came out besides a strangled scream. She tasted blood in her mouth and knew she'd bitten her tongue.

"You can and you must. Once you find your inner calm, Flora can rejoin herself. You must find it, or we will fail."

But she couldn't calm. She tried to separate herself—to not feel—but her will was slipping away.

Then she felt it. The edge of darkness attaching itself to her soul, and her body went still. The evil feeding off her was finding a new way to attack. It was there, pushing at the corners of her mind. Pushing its way inside her and settling in as if it belonged. And now she sensed two consciousnesses peering through her eyes.

Sloane concentrated, focusing on the being floating inside her mind. Wicked laughter bounced around her head, and for a moment she saw into the creature's soul. It was made of hatred, impure thoughts, and acts so violent if made Sloane's stomach churn. This being, so full of sin and debauchery was inside her, clawing at her brain and trying to take hold. It wanted to use her body to do all the evil deeds it dreamed of. She felt herself being pushed to the side as the evil half of Flora settled with a contented sigh.

Sloane's mouth was open but she couldn't scream out loud, only in her mind. Where no one could hear her. And no one cared.

The ghost was now inside her. She was a host for the darkness, and she couldn't let that happen. Sloane knew she had to free herself. She had to do what Steph had said. She focused on herself and let go.

And suddenly she was free. Nothing was holding her down. She was free of the fear of becoming like Flora and ending her days alone and tortured by Michael's loss. She was free of her hatred and her jealousy.

But she was also free of everything holding her to this earth.

She felt herself drifting away. She floated above her body where neither ghost could lay claim to her. The pain was gone. The fear. She was no longer real. No longer part of that torture which had filled her body. She was just the essence of Sloane.

Opening her senses, she looked down at the scene below her. She could see herself, drool dripping from her mouth as her body shook, her eyes open and glassy. Whitney had dropped Steph's hands and was draped across the body, sobbing. Steph sat back on her heels, her hands at her side, a look of shocked bewilderment on her face, though Sloane couldn't tell why.

There was nothing to be sad about. She felt free and more alive than she had since before Michael died.

A light shone through the window, catching her attention. A beam of light, like a spotlight shining from the sun.

As she watched, the light shimmered and formed into the shape of a man. A man she knew. His golden hair was mussed and fell into his eyes, just the way she remembered. He smiled and she felt joy radiate from him.

"Come, Sloane," Michael said, holding out a hand. "Are you ready?"

"Ready for what?" Sloane asked.

Michael raised one brow as if the answer was obvious.

Sloane looked at Michael, then down at her body lying in the circle of salt.

"Oh, I let go too much, didn't I?"

"You were never one to do things half way." Michael winked, his hand still outstretched. "Now, are you coming?"

"But what about…"

Sloane didn't get to finish her thought. There was a frantic pounding of feet on the stairs and the door to the bedroom burst open as Jonah rushed into the room, Brian and Kevin at his heels.

"No!" It was a guttural cry. An anguished sob. He rushed across the room, ripping Whitney off her body and dislodging the rose quartz.

"Stay back." Steph held up a hand to ward him off, but though Brian and Kevin backed into the hall, Jonah didn't listen. With the speed and expertise of one trained for trauma, he began the rescue breaths and chest compressions of CPR. And he wasn't gentle about it. Sloane winced, a pain jabbing her in the side. Had he just broken her rib?

"Jonah?" Sloane whispered. She reached a hand out to touch him, but there was something keeping her suspended. She couldn't get to him.

"Sloane, I said come with me now." Michael's tone was stern, and Sloane turned to look at him in shock. Had he just called her like he would a dog? He'd never talk to her like that. Not at a moment like this.

"This isn't right." She tried to sort through her thoughts. "You said good bye. You said I wouldn't see you again, but now you're here."

She studied him, taking in the sudden scowl marring his features, and began to see the imperfections. It was like someone had tried to recreate him from her best memories but had gotten the details wrong. He would never stand like that, so straight and without a slouch. His eyes were blue, but not quite the right shade and the way he held his hands now in tight fists against his side as if he wanted to strike her was completely against all he'd ever been.

"You're not real," Sloane said. "Who are you?"

"Who do you think I am?" Michael growled.

"The demon inside me." Sloane suddenly understood. "You aren't happy with my body. You need my soul to survive. But I won't give it to you. I have something to live for. I am more than what you want me to be."

With her entire essence, she willed her heart to beat and felt herself drawn like water down a tube, back into herself. She gasped, drawing breath into her stale lungs, as her eyes flew open.

"Jonah." She reached up, gripping his arm like a life-line.

"Steph!" Jonah yelled. "Finish the ceremony. I won't be able to bring her back again."

"Flora." Steph's voice was hoarse with shock but she pulled herself back together. "It's time. You must do this."

Flora stepped forward, but Sloane could tell she wanted to flee. The spirit looked like she was in shock, and she fidgeted with the collar of her high-necked gown.

"You never could face me." The evil voice came from Sloane's mouth, but it wasn't her own. "You wouldn't even believe I was a part of you before, there's no way you'd welcome me back inside you now. I'm stronger than you could ever hope to be."

Standing, Stephanie withdrew a short double-edged dagger that Sloane vaguely recognized as an Athame. With a sharp, jabbing motion, she stabbed the knife into Flora's chest. When she withdrew the knife, there was a gaping black hole where Flora's heart would have been.

"Go," Steph said. "Join with yourself and become the presence you were meant to be."

Flora stumbled and fell forward, her body misting as she dissolved into Sloane's prone form.

Sloane immediately felt a change inside her, as if a

battle was erupting in her very soul. Polar opposites waged a war. At once Sloane felt clean, then dirty. Sick, then healthy. Happy, but sad. Heat seared through her veins, instantly replaced by an icy cold sensation that made her teeth chatter. She was so light she felt herself begin to lift off the floor, only to slam down like a heavy brick. Power surged through her, followed by a wave of weakness that made her want to cry.

She could feel herself splitting in two, as if she was becoming two separate people. Neither one of them felt right though. Her heart beat slowed again as it was severed, one side being pulled toward a dark pit of evil, the other anchored in place by something. She couldn't focus enough to figure out what.

A voice called her name. A deep voice she recognized, and that made her feel like everything was possible. Her heart beat slowed even more, a sporadic thump…pause…thump…pause…pause. She felt a hand on hers, twining strong fingers through her own. She tried lifting her hand to see who was there but couldn't find the energy. It didn't matter. She knew who it was.

"Sloane. It's Jonah. Come back to me. Please, Sloane. I need you. No matter what you think of me, I need you in my life."

Love surged through her, and she reached for him, feeling his emotions pour into her. His love gave her strength.

Using every ounce of her power, Sloane fed the energy inside her into the half of the spirit that was Flora, strengthening the old woman and giving her hope.

Deep in the shadowy recesses of her mind, Sloane felt herself combining with Flora. She felt the woman begin to fight even as Sloane's energy was all but depleted.

The evil entity clawed at the darkness, desperately trying to hold itself together, but Flora held all of Sloane's love for Jonah and his love for her, plus Flora's love for her husband and son. That power was too strong for anything evil to survive.

There was a stillness, like the hazy moment between a lightning strike and the boom of thunder, then with a scream of denial, Sloane felt the two halves of the ghost fuse together. White hot pain shot through the center of her chest, just above her heart, and Sloane screamed, her voice going hoarse as she felt the abused organ skip a beat then stop as the world went black.

Sloane resurfaced as though coming up from holding her breath under water for too long. She coughed, gasping for each lungful of air. Her eyes opened, and she stared into the bathroom. Rin was there. She could see her through the mirror, banging against the glass. Trying to get out.

"The mirror," she croaked, trying to push herself to her feet. Her arms were weak and though she tried, she couldn't rise.

"Sloane, stay down," Jonah coaxed. "You need to…"

"No," Sloane yelled, pushing him away. "The mirror!"

"My wife. She's still in the mirror!" Brian finally understood, rushing toward the bathroom. "I can see her. She's there. Rin! Can you hear me?"

Brian pounded his fist on the glass, tears streaming down his face.

Without hesitation, Jonah strode into the bathroom.

He glanced around, before reaching for the towel rack. With one powerful pull, he yanked it off the wall.

"Don't," Brian shrieked. "If the mirror is gone, she'll never get out."

Either Jonah didn't hear, or he wasn't listening. He swung the towel bar like a baseball bat, striking the center of the mirror. The glass cracked but didn't shatter like Sloane expected. It spider-webbed out from the center, appearing like a thousand-piece jigsaw puzzle. Jonah reached one hand out and pulled the circular shard in the very center out, tossing it behind him. Then shoved his entire arm up to his shoulder into the wall.

It was like watching a magic show where someone steps through a wall or hides behind a small tree, half of them disappearing from view with the rest remaining in plain sight. Jonah's arm, then his shoulder and head disappeared from view. Sloane wanted to scream at him to stop. He would be stuck in there, too! Before she could get the words out, she saw the muscles clench in his lower back, and he pulled back, slowly coming through the mirror, with a very pale, very pregnant, woman in his arms.

"Rin!" The hoarse cry seemed to rip from Brian's throat as he took his wife's limp body into his arms.

Chapter Fourteen

"Is everyone okay?" Sloane croaked.

"You would ask that." Steph mopped her brow with the back of her hand. It was quite possibly the most distraught Sloane had ever seen her look. "Jonah, that was very stupid of you." She shook her finger at him. "What if you hadn't been able to get back when you went through that mirror? How could I have lived with only half a nephew?"

"Although it falls into the 'don't-try-this-at-home' realm, what can I say? It worked." He gave a half smile, relief written all over his face.

Brian and Rin were already gone. He wanted her examined by a doctor, and they had the little matter to clear up of him being charged with her disappearance. Sloane wondered what story they would concoct to explain her absence.

"You didn't have to come back, Jonah. I had the whole situation under control," Sloane said, gasping and trying to sit up. When her head spun, she slumped back down. Steph and Whitney each took one of her hands and helped her to a seated position. "Ouch. Ok, I lied. I'm glad you came back."

"You might have bruised ribs, but at least I don't think they're broken. He *did* save your life, you know," Whitney said. "So give him a fricking break. And make him buy you dinner. You should definitely get dinner out of this."

"Of course I'll buy you dinner." Jonah sighed.

Sloane did a mental check. She felt like every inch of her body was bruised, and she was weaker than she'd been since the Wisconsin incident, but she didn't feel like she had recently been mostly dead.

With their help, Sloane managed to get on her feet. She let the peaceful calm of the house sink into her aching bones. Everything was quiet. Jonah held out his arms and to hell with everything else, she accepted his invitation and wrapped her arms around him, sinking into his chest and closing her eyes. His cotton shirt was warm against her cheek, and he smelled like fresh scented soap and Jonah. Basically, he felt and smelled like home.

****

One Month Later

"Cheers to a happy ending and new beginnings!" Brian held up a glass of champagne Sloane never would have been able to afford.

The roar of the ocean. The crackle of the fire. The sand in their toes. The huge *FOR SALE* sign behind them.

Brian and Rin held hands, and she giggled as she sipped her non-alcoholic beverage. She really was a beautiful woman. And yet Jonah's eyes never strayed to Rin or to Whitney who was sitting on Kevin's lap in a chair beside the fire.

"Enjoy that now," Rin teased Whitney. "When you're as big as me, you won't have that option."

"That's right, soon I'll have two beautiful girls to bounce on my lap." Brian rubbed her Buddha belly.

His wife's cheeks flushed, and she gave her

husband that *you're-a-goofball* look.

After getting a clean bill of health from the doctor and Brian's name cleared, the couple decided the house wasn't for them. And guess who got to list it?

Sloane had potential buyers lined up for showings every day this week. The local newspaper had run a story about Flora and her husband and how a local couple had to make the sad decision to sell their haunted house. With the evil half of Flora gone, the whole feeling of the house had changed. Instead of seeming so full of anguish, it now was blooming with hope.

Still, she understood why Brian and Rin wouldn't want to stay. Bad memories were bad memories, no matter that the outcome was good.

Brian and Rin couldn't wait to start their new family…in an UN-haunted house.

"Sloane, you're sure that new house you found us really doesn't have any ghosts?"

All eyes turned to Sloane at Rin's question. Even Kevin and Whitney looked curious.

"I don't want any stinking ghosts watching us have sex," Brian added. "'Cause if I'm in bed and Rin and I are getting all funky and some Casper pops in the room spying or something, I will seriously—Lose. My. Shit."

"That will never happen. I can promise you," Jonah said. "Your sex life is too stupid for even a ghost to want to see."

"Look, cross my heart, hope to die, stick a needle in my eye. It's not haunted," Sloane assured him. "I even had Aunt Steph double check before she drove back home."

Sloane faked a genuine smile, but the last words

Steph had spoken before climbing into her car were still haunting her. "Next time we meet will be under very different circumstances. Be prepared." The old lady was always cryptic, but Sloane was sure she'd meant every word she spoke. What would happen the next time they met?

Rin heaved a sigh of relief pulling Sloane out of her worrisome fog.

With a clap on his buddy's shoulder, Jonah tipped up his beer. "Best of luck in your new pad, man. But remember, there's never a guarantee in life." Everyone went quiet. "But at least you know 'who-you-gonna-call' if anything does happen."

"Sloane Osborne!" Whitney began singing Sloane's name in the well-known theme song, and it broke the tension and everyone laughed. But Sloane knew what he meant.

"And from what I can see between you two"— Brian pointed to Sloane and Jonah—"I say, quit stalling and get going on your own happiness now."

Before the bantering got out of control, Sloane grabbed Jonah's hand. "C'mon, let's take a walk." If she'd learned one thing from losing Michael, it was that time was short. There was no time for resentment and petty arguments. After Michael died, she'd prided herself on saying, "I'm a happy loner." And she was. But times change.

It was time to embrace her real feelings. This man made butterflies go crazy inside her whenever he was around, and right now he wasn't running. He was right next to her, holding her hand as they walked down the beach. She stood on her tiptoes and touched her lips to his. When she wrapped her arms around his back, he moaned, bear hugging her right back. "I missed you, Jonah. And it hurt. But I don't care where you were. I only care that you came back and you're here now."

"You sure?" he asked.

I love him. I loved Michael too, but never this much. It felt like an insult to Michael's memory, but she couldn't help how she felt. She nodded.

"I was a coward, Sloane. I tried to go back to D.C., I really did. But more because I am afraid of losing you, so it seems like it would be easier to just leave then deal with the consequences of what we did. I know that sounds completely stupid. But then I felt you—here." He tapped his heart. "I knew you needed me, and I turned around."

"What are you afraid of?" She ran her hands through his hair and inhaled his earthy delicious scent. So strong. So manly and divine.

"I have a new assignment. It's dangerous. Deep undercover and I'll be gone a while. I don't know how long. And I have to pretend I'm married." He fished a large Masonic ring she'd seen before out of pocket. "I can't drag you into a relationship with me. With my job and the risks. It's not fair to you."

Now she was mad. Who was he to decide what was fair for her. But pretend he's married? To who?

Then it hit her like a ten-foot wave.

He was going undercover with that blonde snot. And just how far did one go to "pretend" they were married for the sake of an important case for the mighty FBI? "Can't I be your partner?"

Jonah rustled her hair. "I'm crazy about you. Do you know that? But no, that's not gonna happen."

A warmth rushed through her body. She'd worry

about the blonde box of rocks later. Now was now. "How long can you stay?" She wanted to hop in her car and take a three-week road trip, hitting up cheesy motels and making love every night. Someone else could sell this house.

"Truth is…" he started. "Ok, the thing is…I have to leave in a few hours. And I don't know—"

"You don't know how long you'll be gone," she finished his sentence. "I get it. I really do. Let's say we say to hell with tomorrow, let's have fun tonight. Because every time I get to be with you, my directionless life seems back on track. Tonight I want to be your Bonnie. I want to at least pretend to be your partner in crime."

"So you want to rob gas stations and kill people?" He grinned, pulling her close.

Sloane punched him in the arm. He knew what she meant.

He brushed her bangs away from her eyes. "Then let's get out of here." He winked. "I'm sure everyone on the beach will understand."

****

One week later, Sloane put a *SOLD* sticker over her *FOR SALE* sign and sat on the Flora's front porch for the last time. There had been no trace of Flora since that night with Steph and the new buyers bought the house for the story more than for the possibility of ghosts. They loved the tale of true love that pieced together a broken family.

A creaking sound from behind her made her jerk around to look. The empty rocking chair on the front porch was moving.

By itself.

Suddenly, the rocking chair next to it began to move, too. Both rocking chairs kept a steady pace in harmony with each other.

"Flora? Samuel?"

She couldn't see them. But they were there.

"So you're staying then?"

The chairs stopped rocking.

So, she'd sold another legit haunted house. The new owners could never appreciate the good juju from having these two mates here to watch over them.

Everything would be okay. Her phone dinged.

A text from Jonah.

Last time I'll be able to text from this phone number. I wish I could go with you on your next ghost adventure. And if not me, I wish it was Whitney. You know you have a good friend when she practically crawls on the ceiling and is still normal. Too bad she's pregnant! lol I crack myself up. If you don't wait for me, I get it. But I am yours. If you want me.

Oh she wanted him. He had no idea how much she wanted him.

A word about the authors…

Kat Green is the alias of authors KAT de Falla and Rachel GREEN.

Rachel Green has always believed in ghosts but saw her first full body apparition while working at an old movie theatre in college. When she met Kat de Falla at a writers' workshop, she knew she'd met a kindred spirit—one who was also sensitive to the hereafter. And after bonding on a few ghost adventures, Kat Green was born.

Kat de Falla lived in a haunted house for too long. When things really heated up, she had several paranormal teams investigate, but things only got worse. When her mother suggested they contact a shaman, one agreed to come, saying she had been waiting for Kat's call. The home was cleansed and sold. When she paired up with Rachel Green, the idea of co-writing a book with a paranormal real estate agent seemed perfect.

Sloane Osborne and the Haunts for Sale series was born.

Find out more at: www.hauntsforsale.com

Follow Author Kat Green on Facebook and @hauntsforsale on Twitter.